Journeys End
And
Other Stories

J A Peto

Published in 2013 by FeedARead.com Publishing –
Arts Council funded
Copyright © J A Peto.

The author or authors assert their moral right under the Copyright, Designs and Patents Act, 1988, to be identified as the author or authors of this work.

All Rights reserved. No part of this publication may be reproduced, copied, stored in a retrieval system, or transmitted, in any form or by any means, without the prior written consent of the copyright holder, nor be otherwise circulated in any form of binding or cover other than that in which it is published and without a similar condition being imposed on the subsequent purchaser.

A CIP catalogue record for this title is available from the British Library.

**Specially dedicated to Lee and family
You have not only made my
Christmases special, you've helped me
more than you will ever realise**

**Cheer Bruv
Love you loads**

Journeys End

At the Jefferson space station, in the cheapest of the four tourist bars, and old man sat on a stool.
There were two empty glasses in front of him. As he waited for the bartended to refill them, his eyes turned to the small TV in he corner. It was showing the network news, which covered stories through out the solar system. The newsreader's face wore a sympathetic expression, so it was bad news, but the bar was too noisy to make out her actual words.
The picture on the screen changed to an image of a ship flying. It was a large cruiser, lights sparkling. It was the replaced by a picture of the same ship, but now with a burnt out hull. The words 'no survivors' flashed up on the screen. At that moment, another, smaller, ship came into sight, before the picture flashed back to the newscaster in the studio.
The old man stared at the screen in horror.
"No," he croaked. "It's too soon." Suddenly he shouted, "Too soon."
He threw a gold disk on the bar and stormed out.
The barman picked up the gold disc and sneered.
"Earth Tribe," he said in disgust.
"Why do you let them in?" asked the man sitting in front of him.
"Law. They should be locked up if you ask me. Instead the Council pander to them."
He threw the gold disc into a bottle, on the back of the bar, which already contained a few others and then went to serve another customer.

The old man walked up to the ticket counter at the shuttle station. According to the departure list, there were three ships heading out of the system that night. The Mercado, colonist supply ship, would be travelling the furthest away. With luck, once it docked at Centari Seven, he could get another ship straight out to the next sector.

He booked a seat on the large ship and made his way to the departure area. His docking shuttle would depart in twenty minutes. As he waited, he took out a dog eared notebook from his pocket and began flicking through the pages.

"Too soon," he kept muttering.

A few moments later he walked over to a Vidi booth. Quickly, he inserted a disc and punched in a number. After a moment or two the screen cleared and an elderly man with a bald head looked back at him.

"Jack?" The man looked at him in shock.

"Marty, don't talk, listen, it's started."

"But it can't. That's not for…"

"No. It's started, now. There was a ship, the Galactic Reef, burnt out with no survivors. Guess who was orbiting."

"Oh my God."

"Listen, I'm out of here. I'm getting as far away as possible. I don't know what to say, suggest even. Just…be careful."

"I will. Take care of yourself Jack."

"You too."

The old man pushed the disconnect button and walked back to his terminal. He joined the line of people entering the dock shuttles, small ships that would take them to the Mercado, orbiting above them.

The only seat he had been able to secure was in the low section. There were no faux windows, only cage like seats. Each structure was in two sections, eight seats in section and there were twelve structures in each quarter of the ship. Jack was in Port Aft, structure seven, section one They were designed in such a way that each section could convert into its own life pod. There was one attendant for each structure. The people in low section where only short stay. The ship would stop at several ports on its way and low passengers usually hopped from ship to ship, depending on their destination.

Jack looked at his fellow passengers.

The large man sitting in front of him was obviously a station medic. You could always tell. Not only by the red triangle on their uniforms, but also they tended to sleep throughout the journey, as it was the only break they got.

Two, a smartly dressed man and woman, looked like business people on their way to a meeting. They sat talking quietly, while referring to small screen placed in front of them. They had little interest in their fellow travellers.

Two teenagers sat opposite him; again one male and one female. As he listened to them chatter, he realised they were students on an astronomy course and on the way to a week of lectures.

Towards the back was a very smart looking woman, possibly mid fifties or even early sixties, who looked out of place down here. She definitely looked like she belonged in a long stay berth or even a cabin. These seats were definitely at the cheaper end of the ship.

He looked at the attendant, a middle aged man. He looked bored with his job and as if his mind were on other things, but tried not to show it. He was trying to

be friendly, helpful and caring, just as the company logo promised.
Jack sat back and let his mind drift.

The attendant looked over at the old man. Earth Tribe, he thought, didn't see many of them around these days. You could always tell them. They had no data implants, wore strange clothes and paid in gold discs. They refused to be any part of the computer link up. They believed in privacy in a big way.
As far as he, Steadman, was concerned, good luck to them. He himself had five implants. He could talk to any of his friends, and they him, just by thought. He was also linked to the local library section and movie channels. Without question, his favourite was the interactive porn channel, which was why he couldn't wait for this shift to be over and he could return to his quarters.
Steadman sighed and began going through his checklist, in preparation for the Journey.

Jack leaned back in his chair and tried to recalculate. What had happened? Why was it happening again so soon? He felt frustrated by his age and failing strength. There was nothing he could do now, not really. The chance for that had been years ago and they had blown it. Now no one would believe an old man, and an Earth Tribe one at that.

Most of the twenty six hour flight was uneventful. There were movie screens and music channels that those without implants could partake of. There were regular meals dispensed by a box in front of each chair and a small bar that ran into both sections, which the attendant sat behind.

The two business travellers had spent quite lot of time at the bar, but had now returned to their chairs, as had most of the other passengers. The only other regular mover was the young female student who, possibly through nerves as this was her first major ship flight, spent much of her time going to the small bathroom set at the back of the section.

Suddenly a resounding bass sounded and the ship juddered. Jack and a few of the others looked up in shock.

Jack turned to the steward.

"What was that?" he demanded. "It sounded like the engines stopping."

The steward glared at the old man and then turned to the other passengers. Once more he beamed his bright smile.

"As you may remember, your seats are also designed to be you protective shell. Many of you may feel more secure if you re-engage your safety harness."

There was a sudden flurry of activity as people did so. Except, noted the old man, the woman at the back of the section in the last chair. She had steadfastly refused to remove hers, except to go to the bathroom, which she had done once in twenty four hours. He didn't know how she could stand it. Although he liked to sit for a while, he soon got stir crazy and had to prowl; even if it only meant a trip to the rest room or bar.

The steward resumed his reassuring talk. "If the amber safety light comes on, then that means you must stay in your seats. For your safety, harnesses will not disengage while the amber light is on. If the amber light begins to flash, it means that, as a safety precaution, the two compartments will divide. Once it has stopped flashing and the light has returned to green, then the cabins will become joined once more."

Several people pulled on their harnesses, to check the pulling capacity. Others looked dubiously at the communicating doorway, that could apparently seal itself shut in two places and allegedly stay air tight. The steward's expression became even more reassuring. "In the event of the flashing amber light turns to red, the two cabins will be separately ejected from the ship. Once at a safe distance, they will set a course for other pods, ships, stations or planets that they can pick up on radar. Each pod is equipped with its own repeating distress signal (which gives the co-ordinates of where you are now and where you are heading), as well as a limited food and water supply. Although you will need to ration, there is enough to last a few weeks. Each chair contains that person's rations. There are, however, emergency supplies situated above the doorway in each pod, which I, or the designated passenger in the second pod, will dispense should the need arise. Remember to stay cool and calm until we are picked up by the rescue services."

Jack snorted. "Rescue services, hah."

The attendant gave him another frosty look. "I don't think there is any need to take that attitude, sir. This is just a minor fault. It will be fixed soon..."

"No it won't. You won't hear from the captain. You haven't yet have you? And you and I both know that someone should have contacted you the moment there was a problem. But not only is the radio blanketed, your visuals are giving you no help either. They're just telling you to sit tight and wait. That's never happened before has it?" Jack looked at the attendant questioningly.

Steadman's face showed only to plainly the truth of the old man's words, but still he battled to avoid panic.

"Actually, sir, there are certain scenarios we are trained to deal with in just this way. Someone may have tried to manipulate the ship, or the radio frequencies. Whatever the problem is, we will be informed of our appropriate course of action in the next few moments, I'm sure."

His reassuring grin had faltered somewhat, but he tried to bounce it back up. Instead he realised that the entire compartment was staring at with suspicion and, in some cases, growing panic.

"Now, please everyone, just remain calm." He turned to Jack. "I really must ask that you not confer your own anxieties on the rest of the passengers. I understand that you may be a little worried…"

Jack burst out laughing. It took a few moments to bring himself under control. When he did, he sat back in his seat.

He smiled and said, "I'm not worried. I know what's going to happen. I thought I had mad it out in time, but it's all going a lot faster now. I should have realised it would."

Some of the other passengers gave him a look to suggest that perhaps he wasn't as level headed as they had thought a few moments ago.

The attendant smiled and gave them his 'there's always one, isn't there?' look. They smiled back.

The young man sitting in the chair next to Jack gave him a puzzled look. "What do you mean?" he asked. "What's going to happen? Why has everything stopped?"

Jack smiled again without humour. It was a tired, resigned smile. "You wouldn't believe me."

In the seat opposite the young man, the medic sat with his eyes closed. Jack couldn't tell if he was sleeping or pretending to be.

"Put it this way," the young man urged. "I'm not doing anything for a while, and by the way things are going, I don't think any of us. I'd like to know, to see whether you are right are not."

"You wouldn't want me to be right."

"That won't change it. And besides, if you are wrong, it won't matter. And if you're right, at least I'll be prepared."

"No one is prepared. No one believes it could actually happen to them, or anyone else. They think it wouldn't be allowed, that someone would stop it. Same stupid reasons. I thought them myself once."

"Tell me, please."

The old man sighed a long heavy sigh. "Ok, but if I start telling you, I have to finish. You can't know some, you have to know all."

"Oh, yes, that's perfectly understood."

"Then I'd get comfortable, if I were you, it's a long 'un."

The young man sat back in his and let himself be drawn into the sound of the older man's voice.

Jack also sat back and closed his eyes.

"When I was in school," he began. "We had to do a project. We could decide what the project was about, but we had to research it and write a paper about it. My grandfather had an old book, written about places of nautical significant interest. One of the chapters concerned the Bermuda Triangle. I talked to my grandfather about it, and he said that Earth had lots of places that were considered mysterious. He said that there were places were people and their cars vanished; places that became ghost towns over night, all sorts of things. I wrote my project about it. I got an A. And yet, I couldn't forget about it, couldn't stop thinking about it, and I continued to study the phenomenon for many years.

"Through the ages it continued, and, as our boundaries grew, so did these places of doom. Certain planets are off limits because nobody knows what happened to the colonists that were set down there. No amount of scanners or small robots can explain where they are. But it was always relative. Each year, a small plane or sea vessel; later, with space fight, it became the odd ship, or like I say, planet.

"I'm not talking about those hit in asteroid belts, or having a mechanical problem and failing. I'm talking about unexplained disappearances. From 1979 to 1988, only fifteen ships or planes were reported missing over the Bermuda Triangle area. In 1999 it had risen to twenty five. But in 2009, seventy-eight ships went missing, and one of those was the Fledgling, with a passenger list of four hundred and fifty. All over the world, places of that kind were reporting higher than usual disappearances. That was also the year when two colony ships bound for Mars, carrying between them, one million people, lost control of their steering due to production faults. I never counted it at the time, as it wasn't my interest, just an engineering catastrophe. Later I was to remember those system ships.

"The numbers went steadily up and up. I couldn't understand why people were still going to those places. Why weren't there guards to keep people out? Then suddenly, in 2020, it stopped. Well, I mean it went back to the one, maybe two, a year. The number had been so high, it was strange. It was like the entire population had just suddenly become sensible and people kept away from what they didn't understand. But it didn't explain everything. Of course, this was all before I was even born.

"Then in 2050 the same thing started to happen again, only this time it wasn't in Earth's system, it was in Merlin's. The same thing exactly; what were thought to be places of doom, that everyone usually stayed away from, people were going in droves. They must have been, for so many ships and colonists to go missing. But again, nobody was doing anything about it, because people had known for years that these places existed. If they went and got lost, it must be there own fault. But then there was another drop off, as if the number of disappearances had peaked in some way.

"It wasn't until the number of disappearances began steadily rising for three years during my life time, that I realised whatever was happening, it was starting again. That's how I came into it. I started to ask too many questions. I started to find that the people, who had been happy to give me information over the years, suddenly weren't so ready to share. Then I met Nick. We got to talking, and I found that there was a lot more to all this than I had realised."
Jack sighed. Although it had all been so long ago, it seemed like just yesterday he had met the be-spectacled, earnest looking man. He pulled himself together and continued with his tale.
"My project had only been about areas of doom. Nick's interest was suspicious disasters. I asked him what that was. He said that most disasters were natural, i.e. either nature, wear and tear, or a freak accident. But, now and then, political parties, criminals and maniacs would stage a natural disaster. He said most maniacs were happy to be named for their crimes and usually came forward to take responsibility. Political parties and those in it for the money wanted the least amount of people to know as possible.

"He said at first he had only been interested in the natural type. Were there areas that it happened more than others? Were there significant similarities? Could there be a way of predicting these things, by studying the past, star alignments, or changes in the planets themselves? The reason for his change in interest was that the suspicious disasters began to take on a pattern. That was unheard of before. Occasional copycatting was known, but not on this scale.

"Studying the cases, Nick began to realise, with the numbers and the kinds of people involved, it was bigger than any political party or small time organisation. This was more than global, it was interplanetary. The thing that stood out, as far as he was concerned, was the one element that was concurrent with all these disasters was that the victims (those bodies that were said to have been recovered from the wreckage) were cremated before families had a chance to do anything in regards to claiming their loved ones. None of them could confirm that the ashes were the person that the authorities said they were. Officials told the families that records had shown which person was which and that, in case of any infections, the bodies had to be cremated instantly.

"At the same time, there were rumours going on about experiments in various deserts on Earth and Merlin. Nobody knew what was happening, and the governments denied anything sinister but said they were on a need to know basis, and no one outside the experiments needed to know. They would just say they were small experiments in regard for the defence of the planets. Who is going to argue about that, or question the need for secrecy? When you are looking at threats from terrorists from settlements off-world, then you understand that, as few people as possible who knew, the better. All of our security systems have worked that way.

"But for something so small, as the governments insisted, they had a loot of equipment. And the rumour was that the experiments were nothing to do with flight or bombs. It was thought at first that they were containers for aliens the military had caught. But with the amount of containers being sent, there must be thousands of them.

"Eventually it was revealed that the containers were being used for hydroponics experimentation. Each was supposed o be a contained unit that was capable of growing a set fruit, vegetable or fungi. Something they were working on to make sure that the planets could always grow the foods and medicines that they needed. They showed footage of some of the containers, and I must admit that the plants looked healthy, but others still said it was a cover for something else. That there was more going on behind the scenes.

"Nick told me another fact. From 2010 to 2019, people on Earth were told that all family members had to be cremated from then on. There was no more choice of burial, as the planet was too small to cope with it. 2020 cremation law is lifted and the level of suspicious disasters and mysterious disappearances on Earth returned to its original level. In 2047, the Merlin government say that due to the expansion of the human race, humans can no longer be buried there and that cremation is the only option.

"The same thing happened in that system that happened on Earth all those years ago. What happened then? Were humans contaminated with something? Were those little tins of dust really our family members? Or were they somewhere else? And if so, where? We started compiling a dossier of where the ships were

found, or were last seen, and where the remains of the ship were sent. We found it was stepped. Each couple of years, during the Earth cycle, the remains were sent to the nearest planet or out-post. As the boundaries grew, these places were further and further from Earth.
"By 2040, our system had a few planets that were colonised, and many out-posts. The human population boomed. A few years later, we crossed into Merlin's System. Earth is the only planet where you may bury your dead if they were born there. Some of the other planets were starting to adopt the same view and were voting against the automatic cremation law. What happens? The people in Merlin's system start disappearing. It was all connected, but in what way? What were they doing with people and why?

"There was more than just Nick and I asking questions now. There were others who had found similar patterns, or had lost family members and wanted to know the truth. So we decided to find out what was happening.
"A man called Keith, who had lost his son in such a manner, had been looking into the machinery aspect of out-posts being set up, to see if we could glean anything from that. He had a map of the most recent out-post, which was where many of the wrecked ships were being sent to."
Jack paused.
The young woman leaned forward and looked at him. Curiosity had replaced her former indifference.
"So what did you discover?"
Jack returned her look and smiled sadly. "All in good time, my dear."
He took a few sips from the water bottle in front of him then settled back in his chair.

Without being aware of it, the other passengers relaxed back in their chairs as the old man continued his tale. "As I said, Keith had a map. He wanted to go and find out what had really happened to his boy. I felt the same. In the end, four of us decided to make the trip. Nick was to fly the small ship, Myself, Keith and a man called Marty (who had also been aware of the growing number of disappearances) would land near the out-post and discover what we could.

"We knew it would be dangerous, but if there was some chance, however small, that Keith's son still lived, we needed to find out. Whatever had happened, we had not been told the truth. If the boy was dead, we needed to know why, how and who was responsible.

"I admit that, in the back of my mind, was the possibility that this was a government cover up into faulty equipment. Ships that should have been replaced years ago, or perhaps violent, renegade pirate ships, that the military were having problems defend the territories from. I could think of no reason they could have for given people ashes that were not those of their loved ones.

"I know now that Keith had some idea of what was occurring, though even he, I'm sure did not know the extent of it. Perhaps it was because of his profession. Being an electrician, I had never thought that deeply about the subject. Keith was a geologist, so he thought about things like that as a matte of course.

"He tried to prepare us, I think, for what was ahead, but we didn't really listen, just nodded. At the time I couldn't understand why he was giving us a lesson on plane formations and just hoped that we would land soon, unnoticed. As we started the journey down, he began to describe the small planet and the various heavenly bodies that surrounded us. He talked about there various elements and why we could or couldn't land on some of them. He kept stressing certain points about the differences between minerals on other planets and those found on Earth and Merlin. And also about the expense of sending supplies from Earth and the outlaying regions into new areas; the difficulty of transporting certain bulk items that would be imperative to human's sent out to colonise. About how few planets, moons or comet have non toxic water, calcium, iron and such.

"Part of my mind must have been on what he was saying, because I found myself preparing to find people dehydrated, toothless and suffering from deficiencies. Then I reasoned that Keith was probably just trying to take my mind off things. After all, we were going to a planet with an installation; not some remote, un-chartered moon. There were at least four hundred workers at the installation. It must be provisioned enough to keep them going through a space storm, which, depending on its size, could cut off planets for some months.

"Keith became silent as we closed in on the planet. We were shielded from the planets radar, thanks to Nick's handiwork. Although we wanted to land outside the installation's radar, we did not want to land so far out that it took weeks to reach the buildings and infiltrate them. We managed to hit fifteen miles from the radar point, which was thirty-five miles from the installation.

"Nick flew the ship back up and out, as we sped across the surface in a terrain vehicle. One mile from the radar point, we hid the vehicle and set out on foot. We nearly got caught twice and the weather was so bad, it took all day. But we made it to a disused underground tunnel point that would lead us into the installation. The tunnel was created when the installation was first being built, in order to transport building equipment, without it being exposed to the outside elements. There were several around the perimeter of the main buildings, this one was the closest to the part of the installation that, from the maps we had studied, seemed the most likely to contain the answers we would need. There we were met by a man called Johnson.

"Johnson believed that the government were using the facility to store nuclear weapons. He was an anti-bomb campaigner. He had agreed to help get Keith, Marty and myself into the facility. He handed Marty a suitcase, said he couldn't help any further and left. I have never seen him since.
"Marty opened the case. Inside were uniforms for top security guards, door passes and code numbers. There were only four, six-digit numbers, so we memorised them, in case we didn't all make it. Then we changed into the uniforms and each pocketed a door pass.
"From the moment we had landed, we had all become silent. We remained silent now. Marty looked at us, I nodded, Keith nodded then Marty nodded in return. He opened the tunnel door leading into the installation proper and we set off.
"We knew where we were going and we looked like what we were, three men with a purpose. Very few people looked at us as we passed. Each seemed preoccupied, or just plain scared.
"We made it as far as we needed to. Marty's friend had done his research well. He had never actually explored the ship, but he knew every inch, every code, through computer genius. Only one area showed on no map anywhere. As far as the computer was concerned, it did not exist, apart from one doorway that the computer

marked as maintenance hatchway 17. According to maintenance records and rosters there was no hatchway 17. The people who worked that floor said it was rarely used, and only then by top security guards. It was not talked about often, and never by Johnson, but over time, he had managed to work out the codes and clearance cards. They could only be used once to get in and out, but it would be enough.

"As we entered the doorway, we knew we had to march right in, as if we owned the place. As if we had every right to be there, but we didn't know what to expect. We were in an airlock hallway connected to a door at the other end. We carried on forward, the door behind us closed. I felt some trepidation but, after a whoosh of steam, the furthest door opened and we entered the section."

The old man paused. His eyes screwed up.

The young man sat eagerly on the edge of his seat. "What was it? What did you see?"
The attendant stood up. "Look, this really is enough. You are trying to cause unnecessary fear. I just won't tolerate it."
"Shh, let him finish."
"No, Sarah, the man's right. Besides, I'm parched. I could do with some refreshment."
The attendant gave an apologetic smile. "I am unable to serve refreshments while the emergency light is on."
Everyone groaned and sat back.
Jack looked at the Attendant. "It's our last Journey. You should open the brandy and have one yourself."
"That's enough I said," Steadman snapped.

As he did so, he realised he was standing, although the lights had said remain seated. He sat down hurriedly and, to show an example, fastened his harness.

"No," said the young girl. "If we have to sit here, in our seats, I want to hear the rest of the story."

The old man looked at her. He leaned back and let his mind drift back.

"The first thing I remember was how bright it was. Most of the installation was that dulled, indoor, light that you get accustomed to while being on a ship or dulled sunned planet. But this room was bright and warm. We were on a gantry above the room. The gang ran along the edges into the centre, where a ladder led down into the middle of the room. Along the upper walls ran computers. Every so often a guard or technician would run scanners across the boards. Johnson had supplied us with these scanners. They were designed to detect any breeches that might be caused by bugs or explosives.

"Mart nodded to me, I was to remain here and glean what I could from above. Marty and Keith would go down and see what they could find out from below.

"I never knew what alerted them that we were there. I had patrolled the gantry twice. I don't know how I managed to keep walking when I could see what was below me. Keith's voice was echoing in my head, telling me about the difficulties in transporting enough water to different planets, as well as minerals.

"Some scientist, mathematician or deranged, insane, logical creature had summarised it as such; each commercial ship held three thousand humans. Each person contained roughly eight pints of fluid in their body, a high percentage of which was water. Sacks of water that could easily be transported.

"It was cargo that would walk onto the ship itself, plus did not need supplies because, by the time they reached their destination, they would be dead and their bodies would be loaded into a glass chamber.

"As the person liquefied, all liquid (as well as any evaporation) was collected into glass runners all around the chamber. Each chamber had a tube which ran into a bottle. This was then heated. The steam was collected by another tube, which then ran into a large glass tank in the centre. The contents of the tank ran through four larger tubes whose destination I could not see as they disappeared from my view.

"I felt sick and heavy with dread and a new sense of loss. Everyone *was* dead. Regardless of what had killed them, this was their outcome. Their bodies had been placed into a chamber and they now supplied this place with the nutrients that Keith said were missing, as well as around twenty five thousand pints of water. That was per ship. To my knowledge alone, five ships had gone missing in the last two years. How many more, smaller, ships had disappeared without comment? I thought again of the Fledgling and the Mar colonist ships. Over one million people used in this way, just from three ships. The real number was higher than could be imagined.

"I was startled from my thoughts by the intruder alarm being sounded. I was just by the door; I managed to jump through before it locked down, and through the corridor in to the main part of the installation. Quick as a flash, I removed my taser and pointed it at the door. 'Intruder alert,' I yelled. 'Everyone away from the door and out through your corridors. Move'

"The people staring at me began to scurry out of entrances. I waited till they were gone then began to

make my way back to the TV. I climbed all day, expecting to get caught any moment. I slept fitfully in a covered ditch for a few hours, but fear drove me on.
"Finally I made it back to the TV. I nearly cried in relief when I saw Marty. 'I was going in five minutes,' he said, and then he did sob. 'Keith?' I asked. Marty shook his head. 'Once the alarm sounded he grabbed a metal thing and began smashing the chambers. They got him.' He gave a big, heavy sigh that seemed to catch in his chest. 'I got through the door just as t was closing.'
"We both climbed into the TV and set off. Marty continued, 'I got here hours ago. I saw the TV... I couldn't get in. I kept thinking, they're in there, waiting for me. I sat behind a rock, planning what I would do. I fell asleep.' Tears fell again, he brushed them away impatiently. 'I woke up a few moments ago. I realised if they *had* found the TV I would be dead. I was just plotting the course before setting out and contacting Nick.' He looked at me. 'If I had not been so scared, I would have left ages ago.'
"I had nodded. 'I thought you were already dead.' He understood. If he had not been here, I would have taken the TV and left without waiting. We didn't speak again until we had left the planet and were far out of its system. Nick asked what had happened. We told him all we had seen. He did not want to believe us. I told him my suspicion that Keith had guessed what was going on and had tried to warn us.
"Nick looked at us. 'The experiments in the desert? The missing people?' I nodded. 'A dry run. A practice.' 'But we can't prove it?' he asked. 'No, we can't prove it. All we can do is tell people, warn them.' 'But they'll never believe us.' 'We have to try.'

"Nick, Marty and I joined Earth tribe. At the time it was large enough to hide three men's identities, yet enable us to travel the stars, meeting people, warning them. Nick died a few years ago. Marty gave up trying to warn anyone when they all treated him like as if he were some mad space bum. And me? I didn't stay still for long. I still tell people, but those that do believe think past is past, all too long ago. I'm just an old man rambling. But it's not a story, it's real."

The young woman looked at him frankly. "Isn't it a little late? If what you say is true we are all about to be killed and fed into machines, why tell us now?"
"Because you wanted to know and because this is my last time of telling it. I've always managed to keep ahead of it. But this time I've left it too late."
"Your meaning?" asked the attendant, in spite of himself.
"It is my fate to return to such a place, only this time as its victim."
"Perhaps they have a kind of sense," said the young man.
"What do you mean?" asked the business woman.
"Well, what's wrong with recycling? As long as it's done properly."
His friend stared at him. "But those people had a right to go home," she cried. "Their families had a right to claim them."
"Even if you are right, there is still a problem with his plan," said an older, female voice.
Jack looked at the woman at the far end of the cabin. "What?"
"We didn't die," said the old woman softly.
The Attendant gave an 'I told you so, perhaps you'll listen to me in future,' purse of his lips.

"Then we should be given a brandy, like the man said, waiting all this time," grumbled the businessman.
"We've been stuck here over an hour."
He moved t unfasten his safety belt irritably. The button depressed but nothing happened.
"Attendant," he snapped.
"Please sir. The emergency light is on. If you will remain in your chair."
The old man sat back and smiled in a grim fashion. The young woman glanced at him and then looked at the front of the cabin, before looking from side to side in horror. A white mist was forming, raising, coming towards them.
"Oh God," she said quietly. She looked back at Jack. The others began to notice the white mist.
"What is it?"
"Are we leaking?"
"It's just decompression. They've detached us and are towing us in. The attendant eyed the mist with worry. "I'm sure Control has everything under…" he swallowed. "Control."
The young woman looked back at Jack. "Help us."
"It's too late." He sat back and let the mist of sleep take him.

There was sensation, feeling, pain in his head. "You were almost right," said a voice above him. Distant, yet close.
He recognised the voice. It was the older woman. She had only spoken one. He realised she had been hidden from view for most of the flight.
"What…" the old man croaked, his mouth and throat sore, dry, unable to finish the sentence.
"What were you wrong about? Well, not so much wrong as out of touch. You see we tried what you

suggested, but it did not work, not properly. The water was substandard, almost lifeless; we had trouble even feeding the plants. But then we realised our mistake."
The old man felt the sensation of being lifted then placed down gently.

"Dead bodies create dead water. We don't know why. The priests would probably say it's because the soul has already gone. Maybe they are right. Either way we need to dehydrate them as much as possible while they are still alive. We can extract much purer water that way." She smiled a cold smile. "Of course, once the body dies and decomposition sets in, we can collect those nutrients and extract further juices. You would be surprised how much vapour will be drawn up by the heat of those chambers."

Jack's view of the upper gantry was obscured as the lid was placed on his glass coffin and it was lifted and slotted into its place. They had laid his head to the side when they had strapped him in, so that he would not drown in his saliva.

He looked through the glass into the next chamber. The student who had looked him so imploringly on the ship lay staring at him.

As he watched, she closed her eyes and tears began to roll don her face. They were collected in grooves, which ran into the drain, before making their way through the pipes and, their final journey, to feed the planet.

Voices in the Dark

Prologue

Eight weeks before the first confirmed report came in, many people suffered a rash.

It wasn't extreme and in some case could be mistaken for bites or a mild case of chicken pox. Because it was so mild, people didn't really take much notice. But then after the rash had gone, a sore would appear on the body; gradually growing.

For most people, after the sore had appeared, it would become covered by a layer of hardened skin which would eventually flake off, leaving unblemished skin underneath. After that, most people were immune from the disease, but for others, they would succumb to the third stage.

Other sores, like the first, would begin to appear on the body. Internally, organs were being slowed or shut down, and the body began to die, due to lack of oxygen reaching the extremities and the brain. That was when the final stage began.

None of us knew who would survive when the first sore appeared. We just had to see if the skin would flake off, or if the whole body would become infected. And maybe that wouldn't have mattered, if the disease or virus had wiped the lot of us out, but it didn't. Not quite.

Electrical pulses in the brain remained somewhat active, if not completely. Although the people were technically dead in most aspects, they refused to lie down. They were driven by a hunger to seek out and attack other humans. Those that were bitten and lived

suffered a reaction that was fatl, and the victim became like its killer. As the weeks went on, very few lived. The number of those infected was so high that any victims they came upon were ripped apart and consumed.
It was the time of the living dead.

September 1st

"I don't know if this is getting out at all, or if there's anyone left to hear it. I guess I don't need to explain that everyone around here is dead. Well, almost. Coz being dead doesn't seem to stop them walking around taking chunks out of people, right?
"Well, anyway, like you, god I hope there *is* a 'you', I'm holed up away and safe. I hope.
"Tonight is the first time in the last two weeks that there hasn't been any explosions or earth tremors. It seems pretty quiet out there, except for our friends. They don't say much, but I can hear them trying to find a way in. But don't you worry folks, I'm sure they would have got me by now if they could. Touch wood.
"There's been no TV for a month now. Mobile phones don't work, no internet and I can't find any other station that's broadcasting. But I don't know if that's because no one is putting out or I'm just not getting the signal. I can pick up a recorded message, urging people not to leave their homes, to barricade themselves in, to store water and conserve food. I wish someone would turn the damn thing off, or it would run out of power or something. You see, my parents listened to that message; they had belief in it, that, if they did what it said, they would be safe.

"Anyway, if you're out there, honk a horn, blow a whistle, sing or put on a track, but let me know. Let me know I'm not alone. Let me know there are other survivors. Please god, don't let me be the only one.
"Now, a little music. For those of you who know my taste, you may be wondering what this was doing in my collection. Well, it was my dad's favourite song. Nuff said."

September 3rd

"...Papa Smurf, you got your ears on?"
"As always Duke. What's the word?"
"Check out (***) on the dial. There's a guy broadcasting. He's not that strong, we're picking him up in patches."
"On it, back in ten."
"Speak to you then, out."

*

"Sir, I'm getting a live radio transmission."
"Have you tracked it?"
"Yes sir, awaiting orders."
"Ok, don't block it, let's see what happens."
"Yes sir."
"Let's see what's out there. And get me transcripts of all that's said. Out."

*

"The thing I wonder about most, is how did it come to this? Not the disease, or virus or plague, but the result of it. I mean, they were putting reports on TV and radio, telling people the only way to destroy those things was to detach or destroy the head. The world is full of armed people; people with guns, bombs, knives, weapons of all kinds. How did it spread so quickly? Why didn't the army, the police, the people, why didn't they win?

"I haven't seen daylight or the outside world in six weeks, only on TV and not even that now. I tried watching movies, but it makes me forget what's happened; then I remember and laugh so hard I don't know if I'll stop; and then the pain kills me, so I stopped watching them.

"Only the music doesn't hurt, so I listen to that instead and talk to you; because while I'm talking, I can know there is a you, and while you're listening, you can know that there's someone out here, and maybe that you're not alone either.

"In an hour or so, I'll check the receiver again and let you know if I hear anything. In the mean time, let's have some more sounds."

*

"Duke, this is Papa Smurf, do you read?"
"Go ahead Papa Smurf."
"I'm picking up his signal clear, which means I'm probably a bit closer than you. Not a happy man, but I'm just so glad to hear another voice."
"I know, Martha cried. Is there any way we can get in touch with him?"
"It'll take some work, but maybe. Even if we can't talk to him directly, we might be able to leave a message. I'll get back to you when I now more."
"Understood, over and out."

"Goldie, this is Papa Smurf, you copy?"
"Hey Papa Smurf, fancy a game of monopoly?"
"Not right now. Looks like we got another lost sheep, on the dial at (***). I want to track his area. Let me know if you get a signal and pass the message down the line."
"Will do Papa Smurf, it'll take a while, tune in around six. Over and out."

*

"Sir, the network is relaying. It's not just one on one chat, information is going up and down the line."
"They're organising. Know what they're up to?"
"Yes sir. We can't get all of it, but they want to cause a distraction. At a certain time, all those surrounding one area are to put there CB's on to PA system and call to the Zom…the enemy, sir. Some of them are trying to get to a local station to get a message out."
"Ok, so now we get to see what they are capable of. Anything else?"
"No sir."
"Good. Out."

September 7th

"Well folks, I tried, but nothing. I strained my ears so hard trying to catch something in that void of white noise. Sometimes I almost thought I did, but it wa just wishful thinking, or tiredness. Although I don't know how I could be tired, there's nothing to do here except read the books I've already read. But I do a lot of thinking, maybe that's why I'm so weary.

"When I was a kid, we used to play out in the park, pretending we were the only ones left. Adventurers. Everything was exciting, scary, fun. But this is no adventure. It's not exciting and the fear of those things is being over taken by the fear of my thoughts.

"Hiding away like a rat in a box. That's not surviving, it's delaying death, not living. Regimenting my time so I feel like I have a purpose. Eating so I stay strong, for what? So that I can eventually starve or go insane?

"All humans are built to have a purpose, but if all humans are gone and there are only these things, what is my purpose? What have I survived for?

"I tell myself there must be a reason. And I can't be the only one. Others had the rash and sore, but they didn't become those things till after they were bitten. I *can't* be the only one. You must be out there somewhere. Even if you can't hear me, you must be out there. After all, the disease, god, nature, whatever caused this, could have just wiped us out. Why did some fight off the disease and not others? Why did it kill those people, why did it make some into contagious monsters and not others? We can't have been left alive just to feed those things. There must be more to it than that.

"They say that in any disaster, children are more likely to survive and for longer, because they are adaptable, able to fit into small spaces and bolt holes. And yet, even as I wish not to be alone, would I hope that any children had survived to inherit this earth? Not if they had to suffer this fear, this horror. I would wish they survived on a paradise island with no monsters, either walking around outside or in their head. But if there is a child listening, I'm sorry we didn't save you from this."

September 15th

"Papa Smurf, this is Goldie."
"Papa Smurf here, go ahead Goldie."
"They made it. They're in the building, locked in tight. They're setting p now. They've set up a radio too. It should reach you on the tower they got. They said they would broadcast out from nine till eleven and then break off. After that, they'll check in with us to see if anyone picked it up. We should know by then if he can hear us."
"What happens if he doesn't respond?"
"They'll just keep trying till he picks it up or someone else does. They're telling anyone out there about both radio signals and the CB chain."
"I know it sounds daft, but this feels...I don't know..."
"Like we're doing something. Yeah, I know. I actually feel excited. Even if we don't manage to contact him, the station will make it easier to contact each other, there won't be so many delays from one end of the chain to the other."
"Fingers crossed, Goldie."
"Fingers crossed, Papa. Over for now."
"Out."

*

"Sir, there's a live message being broadcast on a different station."
"Good. It's getting real chatty out there now. Keep me informed. Over."
"Yes sir. Out."

*

"Message to the radio man, you are not alone; repeat, you are not alone. There are other survivors. Please let us know if you are receiving this signal. Anyone out there listening, there are other survivors. If you can hear this message and you..."

September 16th

"Oh god, yes, I can hear you. I hope to god I'm not dreaming. I have done before, but please, not now.
"Yes folks, a message on the waves, not only to me but to you also. If you can, in around an hours time, try to tune in on the second station. I'm getting it on (***) but if you don't get it straight away, fiddle around. If not, come back to me and I'll be relaying messages. Praise be, I still cannot believe it.
"Folks, if you can get hold of a CB, fireworks, flashing lights, there are people out there looking to hear your voice and for you to hear theirs. We know you got to be careful making noise around those creatures, but if you can, somehow make a signal. Don't be alone, because until I heard that voice answer mine, I was being beaten down by despair. But now I know, really know, that you are out there listening. I know I have a purpose and I know the fight is not over. The fight to live, survive.
"If you were thinking of giving up, don't. Please don't. Find a way, just for a few days, a week, give us time to find each other. If you know morse code or not. Use lights, mirrors, anything. Try your kids walkie talkie or your grandfather's old ham radio set.

"Don't take foolish chances. I mean, if you are safe where you are, then listen when they say don't go out there, but use what's around you. Fire's not a pretty good marker unless you know smoke signals. The whole countries been burning off and on for the last few months. But a flashing light, or waving flags, messages written on buildings, or top storey windows. No one can help you right now, but if we find out where we are and how many we are, maybe we can find a way to do something, and if not…well, we can always listen to the music and know that we are not alone."

September 18th

"Papa Smurf, this is TC, come back."
"This is Papa Smurf. Did you say TC?"
"Ten four. We haven't spoken before, but Goldie talks about you a lot. I guess we all do. I mean, talk about Goldie and the others. Somehow it makes me feel closer, like it's not just voices."
"I know what you mean so n. Your signal is so clear, you sound like you're just down the road."
"This tower has boosted everything. And people are flashing lights and finding CB's and other radios. We can't hear everyone, but it's getting there. We'll be putting a list on air of who we've got, in what areas and how bad the area is. Listen in with a pen and paper, we need you to relay for us to the people who aren't getting the signal."
"Will do. Anything else?"
"No, just tell everyone I said hi, and I look forward to meeting them one day."
"Will do. And TC, I hope we get to speak again soon."

"Sure will Papa Smurf, Goldie says you're a demon to play monopoly with."
"Prepare to lose a lot of money, over."
"Not if I play with my lucky boot, out."

*

"Sir, another two stations have gone on air, and at least twenty five others on wave band radios. Should we block the stations?"
"No. I want them to link up."
"Yes sir."
"So far a hundred out of how many billion? Let them talk. They'll work it out, but let them have this time. Over."
"Yes sir. Out."

September 21st

"Message to the Radioman. At nine tonight station set to communicate directly and update list. Relay is ready, please acknowledge."

*

"Ok ladies and gentlemen, tonight there should be a real treat for us all, if it comes off. At nine o'clock we are attempting a link up between staions, which means you will be able to hear what I hear. It will also mean that, every two hours, if you have a CB or some form of waveband microphone, I should be able to receive your signal too. So if you've been trying to get in touch, don't stop now, keep trying. And remember, even if I can't hear you, those closer to you can.

"I can't believe I'm shaking so much. Even knowing that I have indirectly spoken to some of you and heard your voices, to be able to actually talk to someone…well, don't blame me if it gets a little emotional.

"Seriously though, many of you will be running low on water and food. You will have no option than to make dangerous journeys. So I'm asking you, if you can, wait till nine; grab a pen and make notes. Your area may not come up on the update lists yet, but if it does, we may be able to give you an idea as to anything that maybe useful in your area to go to, or stay away from. And if we don't and you have to brave it, then mine, and everyone else's, thoughts are with you, and we hope you stay safe.

"It may seem that some of you should go off to rescue someone near you. But try to hold back, we need to make plans. There are ways to decoy these creatures. We might not be able to beat them, but if we can out think them, and move around or through them, then we haven't lost either, and we'll have more chance of success. I'm not saying don't help people. I'm saying help them in the way that's safest for you and them. Don't let me lose you all, just when I think I'm finding you.

"Anyway, I'm going to play a few tracks now, while I finish tweaking. Remember, we come back at nine and either way I will have some kind of update for you. Until then, be safe children, be safe."

*

"Radioman, are you there?"
"Oh my god, yes. Can you hear me?"

"Hey, how's it going? The name's TC and right next to me are John and Phil. Say hi guys. (…hey radio, nice to meet you…)"

"This is for real. You know, I wasn't sure if all this would work. How are you all?"

"We're holding up. Got the updated list for you. But first we got the radio set so that you can hear and talk to a few others."

"Really? Oh wow."

"Hey Papa Smurf, you there?"

"Hey TC, Phil, John. Hey Radioman."

"Papa Smurf, I'm guessing that's not your real name."

"It's a long story. I'm in ---- and I've got a relay of six headed north and five southwest. The can't hear either station, but they are so happy. You guys have really improved things for all of us. Until last week, our group thought there were around thirty to forty survivors, now we know there's over a hundred. We may be spread out, but all this is keeping us together. Now, I've got my relay report for those areas. Do you want it now?"

"Yeah, I think we should start on those. Folks, if you have maps out there, try to mark or pin them, so you will have an idea on where each of us is. And remember, bear with us, because some of this is by relay and it might take a little while for all the contacts to finish. But this information is important to all of us. Let's try and get as full a picture as we can. Ok Papa Smurf, give us your areas and names…"

September 27th

"Good morning world. This is your Radioman speaking, and how fine was it to talk to some of you this morning.

"On our updates today, many of you may remember on last nights session, that Mr Preston was complaining about the Zombies ringing the bells at the local monastery. Well it seems the bells were ringing out morse code, well spotted many of you.

"Apparently, the brotherhood are all fine, though they were somewhat confused. They had no real understanding of what was happening until it was almost too late. Surprisingly, all the monks have survived. When it was queried as to how many had had the first rash, it seems that none had. Being recluses, they had not come into contact with the disease.

"Brothers, I understand you have a very old radio, so I hope you can hear me when I say welcome to the survivors club.

"We also have news of three more stations beginning broadcast in the next few hours. Two are confirmed but, as yet, we have not heard ffrom the third group. Our thoughts are with you guys, be safe.

"Ok, in the next two hours I'll be giving out any new names and places we've picked up, as well as any danger zones or calm areas. And remember, if you see any kind of signal, or hear it, let us know. But remember to keep your head down. Don't cause undue interest on where you are, especially if there's not much interest in you at the moment. The longer you can kept those things away from your area, the better.

"Ho...Hold on, I'm getting a signal from our sister station. Hello, Phil, what's up? I see.

"Well, folks, it seems we just got word that our survivors club now includes a light house in ----, they are sending messages as we speak. Yes Phil, I'm here. Oh my god, really?

"Folks, you are not going to believe this...."

*

September 30th

"Sir, they are in contact with the ship."
"And I take it, by that anxious note in your voice, that you think it's a bad thing?"
"Well, sir, I think it's ill advised. They are growing in numbers as it is, and the ship has over a hundred people on it, sir."
"Yes. One hundred people on a ship. A ship they can't port without risking contagion. Also, twenty five old men locked in an old monastery that will die out, unless nature suddenly decides on a few miracles. Soon they will realise there is no grand return of the human race, just isolated pockets, the same as us."
"Sir?"
"Do you know why I request the transcripts?"
"To observe the situation sir."
"No, not observation, for leisure, entertainment, an escape. There are three hundred of us in this state of the art shelter. We can never go up, because down here we are safe from all forms of contagion. Up there, the enemy are not dying. Maybe they will, who knows, but it makes no difference to us. This shelter is the only land we've got. Do you have children?"
"No sir."
"No. We gave up our chance of that for our career, and now that's all we've got. You listen to other people speaking and I read what they say, same as we've always done. We run this place, check this, observe that, but we will die

out just as they will. But while I seem to spend my time on this radio, talking to a drab, self-centred, emotionless dweeb, they laugh, play games, talk, cry, plan. (sigh) You want to nike the enemy and wipe out everything up there, but those transcripts are the only thing I've got that makes all this worth it. Because I don't know if you've realised it, but there is no world, you're not a survivor, you just exist. They at least are still human, not just machines obeying orders. You, me them, we'll all die, but at least they know what it means to live."
"Sir, I..."
"Out."

Queue

'Yes, madam, that's it, right through the gate. Next. Yes, may I help you?'
'Davis Arnold.'
'I'm afraid you are in the wrong queue sir. If you would like to join the one over there. Thank you. Next.'
'Hold on, what do you mean the wrong queue? Are you saying I should be going…down there?'
'Oh no sir, not at all. Suicides don't go…down there. They end up in purgatory. Now, if you don't mind, Next.'
'Excuse me, what do you mean suicide? I didn't commit suicide.'
'I beg your pardon sir, but in fact you did. Several times, according to your file.'
'What? Look, you've got the wrong person. Check again, Davis Arnold, date of birth…'
'Yes sir, I know your details. Look, you are holding up the line. Please join your own queue and I'm sure they will explain it to you.'
'But I didn't commit suicide and I'm not joining any other queue until I speak to someone in charge.'
'Look, sir, I have a lot to get through. I don't have time to explain to everyone why they don't get in. Please join your own queue and I'm sure they'll sort it out.'

'Next.'

'Hello, look the man over there said I had to join this queue, but I really didn't commit suicide.'
'Not to worry sir, I'm sure it will all be sorted out. Now, name?'
'Davis Arnold. I live at...I mean I lived at...'
'That's fine sir. I've got your name here. This is the right queue.'
'But it's wrong, I didn't commit suicide.'
'Says here you are a smoker sir.'
'Yes, what's that got to do with it?'
'Well, from your time frame, there were plenty of warnings. Smoking kills, yet you smoked.'
'Yes, but...'
'And, in fact, you were even advised by doctors and such not to, repeatedly.'
'Yes, but that's not suicide. I mean high cholesterol can kill you eventually.'
'Yes sir, and I see you were warned about that too.'
'For god's... sorry, for goodness sake, everything *can* kill you, it doesn't mean it will. If you didn't do everything that *could* kill you, you wouldn't do anything.'
'There's nothing I can say sir. You were told that smoking would kill you and you did it, you smoked. That is considered suicide.'
'But that's ridiculous.'
'Is it sir? If I gave you this capsule of cyanide, and told you it meant certain death, would you take it?'
'Of course not.'
'Yet you smoked, knowing that each of those cigarettes would lead to your death.'
'No, it's not like that.'
'So tell me sir, what is it like?'
'Well, it's no suicide, is it. I mean you don't commit suicide over twenty years. It's just a habit.'

'Time means nothing here sir. As I said, you were told a certain thing would lead to your death and you did it. Suicide.'

'Look, you know it's going to shorten your life, but that's at the other end. And by the time you are at the other end, it's too late, you're hooked.'

'The other end, sir?'

'Yes. I mean I started smoking at fifteen and I thought, well, who cares if I'm aeighty or a hundred when I die.'

'But you are, in fact, forty seven.'

'Yes, but I didn't expect to be forty seven. And all this is irrelevant anyway. I died in a car crash.'

'Yes sir. According to your file, you had just scarfed down two double cheese burgers, fries and a hot apple pie (regardless of your cholesterol levels) and then decided what you needed to finish it off was a stick full of cancer causing poisons. As you were distracted by first looking for the pack and then lighting it, you ran a red light and then ploughed into a bus.'

'That's right. A car accident. The bus killed me.'

'No sir. If you had given up smoking when advised to, strenuously I might add, by doctors, advertisements on TV, visual warnings on the packets, you would not have been distracted and you would not have died.'

'But for smoking to have killed me, it would have been cancer or whatever.'

'Not according to our rules sir. I told you, if you are told you will die if you do something and you do it, that's suicide.'

'It's preposterous.'

'Ok, look at it this way sir. If you jumped off a cliff, would it matter if it was the long drop onto the rocks below that killed you, or being hit by a passing glider?'

'Either way the *intent* would be there. I didn't *intend* to die.'

'Didn't you sir? Our records show not only smoking and high cholesterol, but also binge drinking, over use of painkillers for subsequent hangovers, frequently using a mobile phone while driving, and at least five instances of unprotected sex with a stranger. All killers sir. Are you sure you wanted to live? Sounds very self destructive to me.'

'Well…I…I…'

'I mean, all these things you've been advised against, yet knowing the consequence is death, you still did them. Ok, it was the cigarette that killed you, but quite honestly sir, it could have been any of them.'

'Yes… but… I'm not sure. I mean, I didn't *feel* suicidal.'

'I think perhaps, deep down, you must have done.'

'Maybe. Maybe I did, but I wasn't really aware of it.'

'I can't help you with that sir. All I can tell you is why you are in this queue. Now, if you don't mind, through the gate. That's it. Next. Yes madam, how can I help?'

'The man over there said I had to join this queue, but I think there's been a mistake.'

'Ok, no problem madam, let's have a look shall we. Name?'

Time

England, May, 1979

<u>Monday</u>

Success at last!
It took more power than I expected, both processors are burnt through, but I think I know what went wrong. As soon as I can replace them, I will try again. But this time it will be longer than a few minutes. But I must be sure the machine can take it. There must be enough power to return. I can't afford to be stranded.
The future may be full of new and diverse inventions, but they will be useless to me and the machine. Tools are only helpful if you know how to use them. Besides, it's doubtful the materials could be used in conjunction with the materials I have now.
After all, who would have dreamed a few years ago that computer processors would be capable of what they are now. 16 bits just on one processor! My old fours aren't even compatible with the units I've just burnt out. In the future, I've no doubt they must be at least double that. The mind boggles. What possibilities are there for a 32 bit machine? What would it be used for. Obviously the department doesn't know what I've been sing the equipment for. They think I'm researching the effect of electrical currents on the planet. That's how it all started years ago, but now? Now. What a funny word to use. Once the machine is perfected, there will be no such thing as now, then or tomorrow.

<u>Tuesday</u>

It's so frustrating, always having to wait for parts or projections. Bu then, soon I won't have to wait for anything. No more being hungry and having to wait over an hour till it's cooked. Either, put it on at two and jump forward to three, or pop back to one and put it on, so when you get back to two it's ready.

But more, so much more. No more catastrophic losses during natural disasters. If an earthquake happens, you just go back to the day or a few days before and evacuate everyone. No murder, because you can go back and prevent it. How can there be a war, go back and stop a dictator rising.

They may say that life would be worse if you went back and killed Hitler, but how can they know that. Besides, tell that to the people who suffered in the concentreation camps.

Although, that does beg the question, if I *do* go that far back and change such a fundamental thing, will it change reality enough that my machine could never be invented? Impossible, I guess, because of paradox. If the machine hadn't been built, I couldn't go back and kill Hitler, so reality would jump back to where it was, which would mean that the machine *was* built. Trying to work it all out is making my brain ache more than a little. Perhaps it's best if I start off with the little things first.

Wednesday

Was up all night thinking about paradoxes. So far I've only gone back and forth by a few minutes. Perhaps the machine won't let me go back to a time where the machine doesn't exist, and only time from that point can be changed.

These are all questions I need to face before I can ell anyone about my discovery. And even then, I'll have to question who I tell, for all men are corruptible, including the governments, men of God and the average Joe. Those I do share my secret with will have to have the same mental makeup as myself. And how could I be sure?
No, perhaps the only way is to keep it to myself. I know the dangers; I cannot be corrupted into using it for gain or world dominance. I don't want to rule the world, I just think it could be a slightly better place. But if I don't tell anyone, how will I expect them to believe me that people need to be evacuated, or that a person is about to be killed? It's all so confusing. Well, I guess that's something I will have to face when it comes to it.

Thursday

I have been reading a lot of material on the theory of time travel and the paradox effect.
There seems to be a lot of argument on the smaller issues, as well as the larger ones. They all seem to agree that the changing of small things can affect the bigger picture, but not all agree on what would result. Some say, because of the paradox effect, time travel is impossible, it would not be allowed to happen. Well, it shows how much they know. I've already proved it can be done; it's just the lengths of travel I need to establish. How far back, or forward, can I go?
And that's another thing, they all argue about the future more than the past. They say the future has yet to be made, so you cannot travel there, it does not exist. Others say that, as most of the future has already been written, the past cannot be changed.

There is a theory that history, for want of a better word, happens no matter what we do. That, if I did indeed go back and kill Hitler, someone else would just have risen in his place. That, if I stop one murder, someone else will just be killed. Is it true? Another theory to test? That's the question really, am I going to interfere?
At the start of all this the answer was yes, but now I'm no longer sure.
Thank god the new equipment has arrived, let the time travel commence.

Friday

Well, that answers everything you need to understand about time travel.
I decided to test my instant dinner theory. After all, there's no point in going off to change the history of man on an empty stomach. I put the beef and potatoes in the oven and went forward an hour. I am now surrounded by the charred remains of my home.
The fire in the kitchen (started by a faulty wire in the cooker switch) spread throughout the house and even down here in my lab. All my research, test results and programs to run the machine are gone. I've still got the machine, most of it, but it's just an expensive piece of junk that I don't know how to work or repair now that most of the important part has been scorched and misshapen.
There's no way I can start again, I wouldn't know where to begin so that's it for me. It's so annoying, if I still had the program I could go back and change it all, but I don't, so I can't.
Why, why, WHY didn't I send out for pizza?

Killer Instinct

It was Bob, I know it was Bob.
It has to be.
There's no one else. We all have alibis. And believe me, the way this has been, I even wondered about myself at times. Could I have done it and not realised? But now, I know. It's definitely Bob.

I know everyone thinks it was me, but it really wasn't. Even Kelly is looking at me strange, and she's supposed to be my best friend.
I don't know who is responsible, although I'm beginning to have my suspicions. God help me, I even suspected Adam for a while, but he wouldn't, I'm sure he wouldn't.
If I could only prove it though. That's going to be the difficulty. No body trusts me. I can see it in their eyes. I know why, it's that rumour Jenny spread about me. She's just a vicious cow. If I didn't already suspect... Well, let's just say that Jenny would be on my list too.

I can't believe it, all this time I thought it was... but now, after what Jenny just told me about Bob, well, it changes everything.
I wondered what Kelly had meant when she said that Bob liked to party in the old fashioned way, and now I know what

she meant. And to think I leant him my tennis balls! I wonder if Chris knows.

Adam and Kelly don't know the half of what is going on.
If only they knew what Bob was really like. What I'm really like. It's a good job I can trust Jenny not gossip. She knows more than anyone. Still, I'm sure at the trial, if it ever gets to it, Bob won't say anything. After all, I had nothing to do with it. Just because they found the earrings and the trout head doesn't mean a thing, anyone could have left them there.
I think I'm safe.
Why in heavens name did Bob do it? It couldn't have been over the lime jelly and Pringle's incident. If Gwendolin had of talked, it would have looked just as bad for her. After all, she was the one who had brought the banjo into things. Mr Gilbert has never been the same.
I really hope it doesn't get to trial. We have to find a way to conceal it all. And I know Jenny, if anyone can do it, she can.

It's a lot easier than you think.

See most people don't like to think too much. They like to think they do. But you have to give them all the clues before hand and then reiterate or re-establish behaviour and thought. For example, you can't just say such and such is the killer. You can't give too many details of the victim to be, yet you must establish the fact that there are secrets, grudges, all sorts of mixed passions running between two people. This can only be done lightly.

After the event you must recall the separate incidents that led to the fate, but that is as establishing killer, victim, means and motive. In between those two times, you must make sure that people repeat these 'Clues' to each other, in confidence, so that no one can really trace where half the rumours come from.

The next step is the actual murder. This isn't just a rapid stab or shot in the dark. It has to look like it could have been an accident. But then it has to be proved that it wasn't. You must have the players in the right places at right time, yet still remember most of your players were also the audience. Physical clues and red herrings must be placed and produced at relevant times.

As an actual motif of the murder, I set a reprise of Gwendolin's party piece (involving the three eggs and bacon trick) she had shared with us two nights before.

With much planning and preparation I managed to conceal a supposedly clumsy murder under what looked like a pole dance malfunction. And, yes, I did remember to make sure that Bob had been seen near the pole three times on the same day, but three different people.

Three people all separately see a man standing next to something over the course of an hour assume he has been there the whole time, when, in fact, he only passed close each time. They saw it as hovering when they discussed it with each other later.

The soon discovered the bump on the back of the head, the trout head, the earring, but I had also removed the banjo this time. Only Chris and Bob would have known about its existence, which would spice up Chris' worry, especially when he saw the smears of lime jelly. I won't tell you where they found crisp crumbs.

This made everyone class Qwendolin into the murder victim. Then thoughts instantly turned to who could have done it. Nobody had an alibi, everyone should be under that first initial suspicion. Everyone must have been able to have done it, that's only fair.

Now you are free to all discuss openly or covertly with other members, Gwendolin's life and, ahem, private aspects.

Next, you choose someone who instantly distrusts the person you have decided is the killer from the outset. It's never overt, but you notice that watchful that comes into their expression, and that the rarely start a conversation with person.

I chose Adam. He and Bob were not close and I think Adam would have like to spend more time with Kelly and couldn't understand her friendship with someone like Bob.

Any, I did the over the top casual question, the raised eyebrows, slightly puzzled look, before mumbling a thanks and walking away, as if lost in thought.

You then covertly produce or raise a point that directly relates to your chosen killer. It is said innocently, as if not relevant to anything, just a puzzling fact. Mine was the disappearance of Bob's sombrero key chain and torch set, which I had secreted away from the scene, but able to be found, with the corresponding wound.

Then what happens is that, there is much thought of those two persons separately, and then you establish the main link. You don't mean to obviously, it's just an odd fragment or sentence that brings two objects together.

In this case it was 'He'll miss it if he can't find it, it was special to him. Gwen bought that back from Mexico for him.' Then walked away.

Always walk away, it leaves people to discuss what you've said without worrying that have to watch what they say. It's their clue, let them discover it, put the pieces together. Everyone says 'Ahh, I see', as if they have now got the missing piece and solved the puzzle.

They haven't solved anything.

I gave them a victim and murderer just by odd, unrelated lines, quizzical looks and the occasional question. And remember, the question has to be asked in an ultra casual off hand way times fifty, these people really need to have it shoved down there throats that you are suspicious of the would-be killer, but that you don't wish to let it be known.

They are the audience. I direct their gaze, what lines to hear, what props to focus on and remember.

It's fantastic, seventeen years I've been doing it. The thing is, about people I mean, is that they don't want certain people to be the victim or killer. They want those that they dislike or distrust.

Why distrust Bob, because his eyebrows are very bushy and meet in the middle. Also, because of his Irish ancestry, when he stands in sunlight, they could easily be described as orange.

Gwendolin not only had the perfect sad smile of a woman holding on to a terrible secret, she had a name that just shouted victim.

The reality was Gwendolin felt no sadness for her secrets, not even the earrings and the trout head. And everyone knew the banjo was her idea in the alleged lime jelly and Pringles incident, and most people didn't even know about the Dayglo' rhinoceros. But, somehow, as soon as I saw her, I knew Gwendolin would fit perfectly into my cast for this year's special.

Bob also had things look bad for him because he showed the wrong emotions at the wrong times. Instead of not caring what people thought, such as Gwen did, he wore a permanent air of furtive shame. When Gwendolin died, he showed no emotion at all, but his eyes became closed, secretive.

I think Chris felt a certain amount of embarrassment, especially as they were his earrings, but either his youth or his sense of inscrutability carried him through.

I must admit, I did worry about Adam for a while because I knew he suspected me for a long time. But I had done a good job with Kelly. She was easier than I had imagined, but the best way to start with her was to mention the things she knew Bob got up to, then have one of te others telling her more stuff.

Kelly and Chris getting together for a chat really worked in my favour, because he admitted to her some of the things Bob was also capable of, but not all of it, by no means.

I could not have planned her looks of growing suspicion any better. They instilled to the others that if she didn't know all about her best friend, what was Bob capable of that they didn't know about.

Poor Bob, who is very susceptible to atmosphere, picked up quite quickly that all eyes were pointing at him, and they weren't very friendly. His closed sense of shame grew and he played his part magnificently.

Don't get me wrong, I love writing the Broadway plays every year, but you can't beat the real thing.

The Right Way

'Is it time?'
'No, not yet.'
'Well how much longer?'
'Just shh will you. Can't hear a thing.'
'I'm going numb.'
'Just stay still.'
'That's what I'm saying, if I don't move soon, I won't be able to.'
'Oh for goodness… Just be quiet.'
'Look, you may be used to all this. I just don't understand why we didn't do it this afternoon.'
'Because. That's all you need to know.'
'It just makes more sense. Why wait till ten minutes till the sun goes down.'
'It is when the vampire is at his weakest.'
'No. Twelve till two, when the sun is at its highest point. That's when SHAM, slide out the coffin, BAM, rip off the lid, and SIZZLE, no more Drac.'
'*Drac?* The greatest undead legend? The master of all masters? The true prince of blood, *Drac*?'
'Sorry. But you know, at the end of the day, he's just a vampire. I mean, I know you're the top geezer when it comes to these old house jobs. I'm more of a modern infestation type. You know, we both get to see the same things. I'll grant you, in some ways you know way more than me on, you know, history, bloodlines, heritage. I don't worry about that sort of thing.'
'That's right, you don't. You, sir, are nothing but a money maker. Gap in the market, that's how you see them, a way to make a profit. You don't understand their inherit evilness, their purpose.'
'Only purpose they got is to feed off each other, spread their disease. One rat's much as another.'

'Finesse dear boy, finesse.'

'Look, out here, old castle, you got your main drac, a few subs he's made and perhaps a living larder of a couple of lost motorists.'

'You really have no respect.'

'I'll tell you what I've got. I've got gangs of them, fighting each other, constant wars. Tower blocks full of them, no go areas. When I find a nest, I let as much daylight in there as possible. Quick and simple. Let 'em fry in the light. Stake if it's needed to pin them down and then, whoosh, natures remedy.'

'I'm sure nature is very grateful. But this is what I'm saying. This is Count Dracula. *The* Count Dracula. He doesn't come under the same heading as your commonplace vampires.'

'Commonplace? I'll have you know…'

'Please, I meant no insult. But you see, urban vampires are in fact hierarchal. There is the patri or matriarch and lessers down the chain.'

'This guy is no different.'

'Yes, he is. And that's rather the point. Vampires, in the most part are its. They are a pyramid scheme, nothing more.'

'First thing he does whenever he rises is follow the same pattern. A man being driven insane; three missing women who are seen at night in nightdresses and various locals being struck down with a mystery virus.'

'What are the very first words you used?'

'What?'

'You said "First thing he does whenever he rises." And there you have it. He rises, again and again. You cannot kill him in the conventional ways because he will always return. You can only find ways to defeat him for a while.'

'Well perhaps if you didn't follow all these stupid rules and regulations, all this ceremony and paraphernalia...'

'Ok, tell me, your urban rats. How many can disperse themselves into mist?'

'Well, one or two are…'

'And enter the minds of animals? Direct human's thoughts over long distances for days, weeks, months?'

'It's more difficult in the built…'

'How many can enslave without shedding a drop of blood? How many will face our grandchildren.'

'But that's it again isn't it, he always gets caught. One way or another he's always destroyed.'

'Ah, no, not destroyed; fended back.'

'And, I mean, how do you know it's the same bloke? I mean it could just be one of them putting on a cloak and just sticking to the stereotype.'

'Stereotype? It's a covenant man! The blood is the life. He doesn't just drink their blood, he drinks their life, sip by sip. Years stripped away and giving him strength, life.'

'He's the worst sort of parasite, pretending to be somehow special, unique.'

'Don't you understand anything? He's an embodiment. Your savage rats run around, ripping out throats, creating drones, they know nothing. Let me tell you, everyone of his victims lifts their throat to him willingly.'

'Oh yes, after he's brainwashed them. I mean, that's acceptable, isn't it.'

'To take away all fear and terror, to give death peacefully, in pleasurable dreams.'

'You see, you're romanticising it. It's still the same crime. He, or it, whatever, steals the living blood from its victims until the point of their death. He sends people insane and destroys communities.'

'You see, that's what makes me so cross.'
'What now?'
'Do you eat chicken?'
'Yes, you know I do.'
'Right, you don't have a farm, but you know a farmer who keeps them. It's ok, the farmer can kill the chickens because they are food. If the chickens all turned on the farmer and started eating him, would you kill the chickens? Or would you say it was just nature?'
'But that's like saying if the chickens have a parasite, the farmer can't destroy it.'
'But he only does so to ensure he can kill it later as food.'
'This has nothing to do with…'
'It has everything to do with it.'
'Look, I just want this over.'
'Yes, and that's a bit of a problem. You see this isn't ten minutes before sunset, run in with a stake. This is the beginning of a battle that will last until dawn.'
'What?'
'It has to. We need him out of his coffin, so we can fill it with holy wafers, so he can't get back in. If we let him get near water he'll sink, freeze and slowly shift towards the castle. It's got to be full stake at dawn, ashes into four vials and sent to the four corners.'
'What?'
'Look, I know your training has been in/out missions, high body counts (no pun intended). This is about being able to sustain a forward attack for a considerable amount of time. Yes, there are rites to perform, ceremonies, spells, whatever you want to call them, because the more you do to eradicate him, the longer he is gone. If you just cut his head off, he'll be back before Christmas.'
'So why are we attacking ten minutes before sundown?'

'We're not attacking him, we're attacking his defences. It will get him up and about pretty quickly. That's when we can get to his coffin and make sure he can't return.'

'How many defences has he got?'

'It's hard to say. Even his non bitten victims will assist him. You may even have doubts yourself.'

'Not me, mate. Seven years field training. They try it, I feel the tickle, but I'm too strong for them.'

'Up until now. Remember what he offers, seduction; whatever that means to the victim. Sexual, drug or darkness, he helps them open doors inside themselves. You might not even know he was doing it.'

'I told you, I can feel it. Ok, after we've done the coffin, what then?'

'There is no then. From the moment we begin this attack, it does not stop. He will be sending all his ammo at us; bats, dogs, people, rats. We will be facing all this, rescuing prisoners and hoping they don't attack us or wander off. If we're still alive at dawn, we attack him just as he tries to return to his coffin. Stake, light, ash, vials. Got it?'

'Ok, look, I get what you're saying. I really do. But why only two of us? I mean how long would it take, really, if we went in, stakes blazing, take out the defence and then…'

'And then what? That's the point. We're not doing all this and then letting him slope off. We've got to keep him occupied, where we know where he is. Hundreds of people, he could jump into any one of them and get them to help him escape.'

'So why has no one blown up the castle while he's…resting in jars?'

'They say it happened once. The whole castle just crumbled and was swallowed into the hill. Two years later some travellers got lost and saw a castle. No one knows when it came back. It was just there. The young man died and the woman died years later in an asylum. She was waiting for her master to come back and claim her.'

'Ok, so what about the coffin? I mean, why mess around with wafers, why not just cover it in gasoline and strike a match.'

'Because the coffin is indestructible, have you never wondered why the thing doesn't burst into flames when he does. It's part of the legend. Did you read any of the material I sent you?'

'Well, there was rather a lot of it. I'm not sure why you chose me to join you on this. I'm not the academic type.'

'Yes, well, I seem to be running out of academically trained assistants these days. I thought perhaps the more physical type might fare better.'

'Exactly how many assistants have you had?'

'That's not important right now. To answer your question; the coffin was said to have been made of the wood from the tree of Judas. It is a supernatural object in its own right. It cannot be cut, burned or in anyway destroyed.'

'Do you really believe that?'

'It's in the official records. I don't see why not. Anyway, it's time. I can hear the servant moving about, which means the trio will be awake in about thirty minutes. We're going to make our way to their chamber.'

'Why them?'

'The rest of the human types don't really work as a team. The trio can be deadly. They're everywhere at once. They are called the trio, but really they are parts of the same creature. It has one motive, to feed on you, to death, while you lay there helpless. That is their true pleasure.'

'Will he rise then?'

'Yes, but he won't come to their aid. They are to protect him, not the other way round. He will be sending out spies to see what we are doing. When he sees us destroying the coffin's safety, he will send his cohorts to defeat us and clear it. We must keep him busy.'

'Ok, got it.'

'So, you are ready then?'

'As I'll ever be.'

'Good luck, slayer.'

'Good luck hunter.'

'

Priceless

Do you know what it's like, just walking in and seeing it? Just there, hanging on a wall, right in front of you. Your heart stops, time stops, your mouth dries. Your brain, not wanting to jinx it, says 'no, it's not it, look for the flaws, look for the tell tale signs. It's just a good fake, that's all.'
But it isn't. You know it isn't.
If it was, it wouldn't be hanging on the wall of some random old woman. It would be shown off, yet in discreet lighting. So at first glance you would say 'Oh my word,' then closer inspection would reveal its true face.
But this? Oh.

There were those, even myself at times, who thought it must have been destroyed, or part of some selfish owners collection, refusing to admit it was stashed in their vault.
There are quite a few of them like that. Just knowing they had something the world coveted was enough. It was enough not to say mine, but to think it.
There were people who collected from certain artists, there were people who collected certain subjects or eras, there were those that collected the very rare and those that collected the priceless.
With this one picture I could name my price to any of them.

It was my granddad who first got me into the business.
Well, I suppose you would call it two businesses.
You see there are two kinds of art dealers, the ones that go to auction houses, galleries, that kind of thing. They know what they are looking for. They hope to make a bit here, a bit there. They know price, what it is worth and what they can get for it. They know how to sell,

which names are in fashion and such. They might choose books, oil paintings or little pieces of porcelain that are worth a small fortune.
Then there is the other type, my type.

Most people think my job is a central heating engineer, which I am. In my grandfather's day, he was a sparks (an electrician if you didn't know). But what we really are, are opportunist dealers.

I go to many, many houses, of all stations. It might be the middle class family, the old lady on restricted means, the family on the dole or even the top end (though that's getting rarer), both as customers, and owners of hidden treasures.

And, in the line of installing the sleek and slim-line, economic and hardwearing radiators and double-boilers, I notice stuff.

You see I have to go into every room. I explain how everything should be boxed up, put out of the way or put in storage, don't matter, but so long as the area I'm working in is clear.

In the initial job assessment, I look for those little rarities that many people have without realising; Aunty Louise's Georgian tea service, a very rare china doll, a first edition of an author of note.

Depending on the object and the customer as to whether I would mention the said piece, and not as you would think.

Take, for example, what I can see as a much sort after piece of earthenware, sitting on a shelf, with junk keys, bits of change and an old battery sitting inside it.

'Alright to move this over there, I don't want to chip it,' I would say.

'Oh yes, that's fine. Though it's not a problem, ugly thing, his mother gave it to us. Don't know why I keep it.'

'I know what you mean, not too keen on browns and oranges myself.'

Two days later, I might mention my daughter and how she's had a hard time of it lately. I say that she's getting married. She won't let me pay for it, but instead she wants her kitchen done up in the same style as the bowl. More subtly put, of course.

This will invariably mean I am given the said bowl to pass on to my daughter. I protest of course, but am persuaded. A few days later I will give them a box of chocolates or a plant or something, from my daughter with a little thank you note.

The thank you will cost me no more than a fiver, but I can make £180 to £300 on the bowl. It maybe ugly, but people are still mad for certain pieces.

Obviously it's not always that easy. I might have to wait six months and then get a 'friend' to do a quiet bit of breaking and entering. They can have the TV, DVD and what not, so long as they get my little item for me. If it's small enough, and I don't think they're very observant, or they have a lot of visitors, I might even slip it into my tool box.

But this, this was something else again.

This wasn't worth a couple of bob, this was worth millions, and I mean ***millions***. And it was just sitting on the wall in some old dear's house.

It had been such a shock, walking and seeing it, that she'd noticed my look.

'Lovely, isn't it,' she smiled. 'My mother found it in the cellar of a house she'd bought. She wasn't too keen on it, but I was, so she let me have it.

She'd have loved it if she'd known how much it was worth, I thought.
I casually glanced around the room.
'Well, you've got lots of bits and bobs; you'll have to pack them away while I get on. That way nothing will get broken.'
'Yes, that's what the plumber said. Though I'm not sure they'll like it.'
'Plumber?' I asked, totally missing the point I should have queried.
'Yes, well, the nice people from the council came round. Said my kitchen and bathroom needed upgrading. And then they said I could have central heating too.'

I'd known it was a council job. I was a good contractor in their eyes and they often sent work my way, so long as my estimates were pretty low and realistic. I just hadn't realised it was a full house job. Had anyone else seen the painting and known what it was worth?
'Would you like a cup of tea?' she asked.
'That would be very kind, thank you.'
My mind was racing along while my mouth was on autopilot.
'Will your kid's come round, give you a hand with the packing?'
'Oh no, bless. I never married. Well, people like me, we don't. It's not fair to the other one, is it, really?'
She potted about getting the cups ready and putting biscuits on a plate.
I nodded absently. My mind had run through the options pretty quickly. There was only one real way of getting hold of that painting and being able to put it up for sale (behind closed doors of course). There was no

way she would willingly part with it, she loved it. And a burglary would mean she would give the description out. A lot of people would suddenly become very interested.

It meant I would have to torch the place after I had removed the painting. It would have to be a proper blazer. No one should see the space where a painting had lived for the last however many decades.

Not a big problem. I could easily knock up a frame of the right size and shove it up so there would be corresponding charred remains, but the painting itself would have to be obliterated.

The problem was, her.

She wasn't the type to go off on holiday. I'd tried to pump her a little on her family and friends, but it seemed like she had no one.

It was sad to say that I couldn't see the fire brigade getting her out in time. But then, an old lady, alone in the world, dying in her sleep from smoke inhalation, there were worse ways to go.

I just had to get it done before the work started in her house.

I looked around again. She really did have a lot of stuff; ornaments, trinkets, pictures, books, all kinds of stuff.

My initial shock at seeing the painting had made me miss the fact that there were some other bits and pieces that were worth a few bob. I wasn't interested in them, but if it wasn't for the painting, I know I would have priced up half the room by now and would have found a good couple of grand.

'You've got quite a collection of bits,' I said. 'Must have taken a few years.'

She sighed. It wasn't sadness, but it was… something.

'Yes. Who'd believe there was so much of it in the world? When I was young, I supposed I was resigned to it. I didn't have a choice, it's what I was. But now, I'm glad. And I've found a place in my heart for each of them. As they found a place for me, I guess.' She smiled.
I smiled back. Dotty old thing, I was thinking.
Idiot.

I've never been superstitious, but I can honestly say, looking back, I did feel something that night.
It all went to plan. Sort of.
The house wasn't raised, but the walls and other pictures were damaged enough that my substitution caused no problems.
She wasn't the first death on my conscience, so I lost little sleep. And, with the painting in my attic, wrapped up, I could afford to take time, and put out a few feelers for the right buyer.
Did I notice things start to go wrong in my life? Not at first. Just thought 'Sod's Law,' then 'Tch, bit of bad luck,' then 'For god's sake, what else?'
It wasn't until I got a call from Terry Masters, from the council, that I realised what I had done.

He told me the job had fallen through; that the old lady had died and that clean up was in progress and that maybe in a few months they would give me a call.
'Shame,' I said. 'Seemed like a sweet old thing.'
'Sweet as a nut and balmy with it,' he replied.
'She didn't seem that bad.'
'She didn't tell you then?'
'Tell me what?'
'What she was.'

It was then that I felt a twinge of unease.
'What do you mean?'
'You must have seen all that stuff she had, ornaments, brick 'a' brack?'
'Well, yeah, I told her she'd have to box it up.'
'So did we. She said she wasn't sure they would like it. It turns out she was a collector of sorts. Well, that's not the right word.'
'What are you on about?'
'She didn't buy that stuff, people gave it to her.'
'What, you mean as presents?'
'Not the sort of present I'd want. It was cursed.'
'What was?'
'All of it. If someone bought something, found something or was given something and then they'd suffer bad luck, they would give it to her.'
'Ha ha.'
'I'm not joking mate. She said that was her job in life, to look after all those things. She said a few times there was a battle of wills amongst the spirits that haunted them, but by and large they were happy to be there.'
'She really was daft then?'
'Daft as a broom.'
'Poor old girl. She said she'd never married, that it wouldn't have been fair, but I never twigged.'
'It's the people that let her believe it that does me.'
My mind started to flick through all the little things that had gone wrong for me lately. Then I dismissed it. Stupid.
'Oh well,' I said. 'At least the local charity shop should do well, the fire didn't destroy everything.'
'Yeah. Right. How did you know that?'
'Oh, well, I'm guessing.' I could have bit my tongue off.

I'd known because I'd followed the story in the local press and news bulletins.
'Yeah, well, funny thing I suppose.'
'What?'
'The van they sent round crashed into traffic lights.'
'It's coincidence.'
'Yeah, well, look, I'd better go. Maybe I'll call you soon.'
It was there, in his voice. I could tell he knew something. He wasn't sure what yet, but the seed had been sown. Me and my big mouth.
So that was another thing that had to be sorted.
Goodbye Terry.

Unfortunately, this time I got caught a little by the fire. I burnt my entire left arm, quite severely and I wasn't able to cover my tracks as well as I normally would. Not surprisingly, the fire at Terry's was put down as suspicious. Hospital records showed I came in with severe burns the same night. It didn't take them long to put two and two together.
While I was being processed at the police station I heard a conversation regarding the charity shop on the corner. It had been flooded out. They'd had to farm out the contents to their other shops while the buildings structure was assessed
Everywhere, I thought. All those cursed objects, they're out there everywhere.
Then, today, I got a letter from my wife. She'd found the painting in the attic. She didn't like it much, but our daughter Stephanie did. She's taken it with her to hang in her front room.
What have I done?

The End of the World

She answered the phone on the second ring.

"Yes?" she snapped irritably.
"It's the end of the world."
"When?"
"Tuesday night. Nine oh five pm"
"See you soon."
"Sure."
She returned the phone to it's cradle.
Well that certainly changed things. She would have to cancel dinner with the Cartrights. Shame. She had been quite looking forward to it. Still, nothing else for it, under the circumstances.
Her eyes swept to the computer. Better get this done now.
She sighed against the futility of it all and once more bent her head to her task.

Quickly she headed into the bedroom. She picked up a cat basket sitting under the window and placed it on the bed.
"Hermy?" she called. "Come on Herm."
A tortoiseshell cat bounded into the room and rubbed against the cat box, before walking in and lying down. She closed the box and grabbed a small holdall. She picked up the cat box, slung the holdall over her shoulder and headed out the door.
As she descended the buildings main staircase, she looked through the small windows. She could see his car parked in the space opposite her side of the tall building.
He flashed his lights to signify he had seen her then switched them off.
Once out of the building, she hurried over to the cruiser and climbed in.
"Hey."

"Hey." As she spoke, she leant back and placed the cat box next to a large Alsatian sitting in the back. She opened the door of the box and Hermy wandered out, climbed on top his carrier.

The man passed her a large paper bag. She opened it and began removing the various burgers, chips and chicken contained within before handing it out.

Chicken nuggets for the man and Hermy. Quarter pounder with cheese for her and three plain burgers for Ketra.

"What time is it?"

"It's ok. We've got two hours yet."

They all became silent as they ate the small feast. Music was quietly playing from the cd player. It was quite a long Cd and covered the last four decades.

After they had all finished eating, she opened the window and picked up the small holdall. She rummaged inside and pulled out a leather tobacco pouch. Reaching in, she pulled out a large joint from inside.

She lit it and leant back, puffing contentedly. She didn't offer the man any. He didn't smoke, but he did not begrudge her the pleasure.

For a moment he sucked noisily from his large cola. Then he looked at her.

"You know, every single one of my friends are married. Some happily, some not so happily. But they've all done it. They've all met that someone that makes them want to stand up and say I choose this person. Above all others I choose them."

He sucked noisily on his straw for a moment then continued.

"I mean at first it didn't matter. You know, one of your mates gets hooked and you all laugh at him and take the piss. But then, suddenly, they all have and they take the piss out of *you*."

She said nothing, knowing there was nothing she could say.

"All around me, everyone finds this person that changes their whole livfe, and it's real. I've seen the pain in my friends. They really love these women."

Another slurp.

"I mean, not all of them. I mean some of them are married to the most incredible women but it doesn't work. He's not happy and I'm thinking 'are you mad? I would give my right arm for what you've got.' But I've never felt that way. Not about anyone."

"But if he's not happy, maybe it's not love. Maybe he hasn't got what you want."

"No. I saw what he was like with her. He wanted her to be his. He was totally smitten. And you should have seen them on their wedding day, totally in love, the pair of them."

"Look, you know what I think."

"Yes, that I'm too fussy. Bt it's not that. It's me. There's something missing in me."

Silently she took another drag on her joint. She felt the same way. Whenever she had been in a relationship, she had been unable to stop looking, and wondering, about others. At times she felt she had been close to love, but deep down she knew there was no such thing as a halfway point, wither you did or you didn't. She never had.

He looked at her. "So how's your nonexistent love life going?"

She grimaced.

He laughed. It was a warm and sympathetic sound. "You too huh?"

She rummaged in her holdall and pulled out a chocolate bar. She broke it in half and gave him a piece.
"Why did you sound so miffed when you answered the phone? 'Yess'," he mimicked.
She laughed. "I was right in the middle of something and four people had interrupted me already."
"well ex-cuse me. End of the world and all that."
"I know."
"talking of which, one hour five minutes left. Hello, looks like trouble."
She followed his gaze. Two very tall policemen were coming towards them.

Andrews and Warrick looked at the cruiser parked outside the block of flats.
The engine was switched off and the two people that could be seen inside looked to be having a conversation.
To Andrews it didn't look very threatening. But a call had come in from one of the tenants that drug crazed weirdo's were selling their dope from the cruiser.
"You sure?" asked warrick.
Call came, got to see to it, otherwise we get the stick."
"Yeah, but I know that geezer. We went to the same school. I see him about. No way he's a drug crazed weirdo."
As they approached the cruiser Andrews caught the wiff of cannabis.
"Drugs are drugs. Come on, let's get it over with." He walked over and beckoned to the driver.
As the man vacated the car and came to stand in front of the vehicle Andrews could see the man wasn't even stoned, let alone drug crazed.

He sighed. "Good evening sir. We've had a report about drug users out here. May I take your name and see your licence."

The man struggled with his own sigh and handed over the docket. As he did, he gave a quick glance to Warrick and nodded.

Warrick returned the nod then walked over to the passenger side and looked inside the vehicle.

He saw a mound of empty burger wrappers, some half filled coke tubs and a couple of unopened bags. They looked like pop corn and cheese puffs.

Sitting in the front was a serious faced woman with shoulder length brown hair. Although she was not what he would describe as drug crazed, her eyes held the unmistakable lowered lids of a cannabis smoker.

In the back seat he saw a large dog sitting next to a cat. Neither looked at him with much interest.

He cleared his throat. "If I could ask you to step out of the car madam."

Blushing slightly she did so.

"Look," she said. "It's not what you think."

"Madam, I'm just doing my job. We had a report, we're just following up."

They came round the front of the car to stand with Andrews and the man.

"As you know," Andrews began. "cannabis is still illegal, especial whilst in possession of a car."

"But he's not smoking it," argued the woman. "I am."

"As you say madam, but I'm afraid I can't take your word for it. I'm going to have to search the vehicle. Also ask you to join us at the station."

She looked at warrick beseechingly. "But it's the end of the world. Can't you just wait?"

"Beg pardon madam?"

The man vent a sigh of frustration. "Look, in exactly…" he looked at his watch. "Forty-five minutes and ten seconds, it will be the end of the word. Can't you just give us that time? We won't go anywhere."
Warrick continued to stare.
Andrews, being an avid surfer of the net, grinned. "You mean the prediction they put up last week? It's not real. They're always saying it's the end of world."
"but what if it really is? What if this time they're right?"
"Sir, I don't think…"
"Look, no one knows what's happening day to day. Can you tell what will happen tomorrow? No one can. But what if there's really no tomorrow?"
The two policemen looked at each other.
"Please," begged the woman. "We won't go anywhere. You ca sit with us. But give us this last forty minutes."
The man looked at his watch. "Thirty nine minutes."
"Sir…"
"Andrews?" warrick turned away and took a few steps to the side.
Andrews joined him and looked at him questioningly. "What do you think?"
"About the end of the world? Come on warrick, they're always predicting it."
"Yeah, but look at them. They haven't moved for over an hour. They've even got their animals sitting there with them. They're just having a last meal and waiting for it. I mean, what harm are they doing?"
"That's not our decision."
"Isn't it? We're supposed to keep the peace. They look pretty peaceful. Can't we just wait? Afterwards we can nick 'em if it comes to it."
"Warrick…"
"Please?"

Andrews sighed. "You're mad."

Warrick grinned. "Cheers man."

Andrews turned back to face the two hovering uncertainly by the van.

"Ok. You've got till ten past nine. After that no arguments."

The woman smiled and warrick could see that when she wasn't so serious, she was quite attractive.

"Thanks," she said with obvious gratitude.

"Yeah, well, it's not over yet. We'll be sitting with you."

The man and woman got back into their seats. Warrick and Andrews went either side of the car and got in.

Andrews shifted in his seat to get more comfortable. As he did so, the large dog sitting between he and warrick, laid its large head on his lap and looked up at him with baleful eyes. Almost against his will, Andrews felt his hand come up and start gently ruffling the dog's head.

Warrick sat back. "You know, I remember when I was a kid, hearing about the end of the world. It was supposed to happen on the following Wednesday. I thought 'great, I won't have to go to school on Thursday.' That was our P.E. day. I hated P.E."

Were you scared?" asked the woman.

"Not really, I was more excited. But then, I was only nine."

"What did you do?"

"Well I told my mum, but she wasn't really interested. I remember arguing with her. I couldn't understand why she was still sending me to school. I said to her 'don't you realise the world will end and you will never see me again. She just laughed. I guess that's when I realised that adults don't really like kids."

The man laughed. For me it was when I found out about Father Christmas, easter bunny and tooth fairy. I mean they went to so much trouble to instill how real it was. Then I found out it was my dad."

"Things seem so simple when you're a kid."

"Tell me. They had also told me about god as well. After I found out about father Christmas, I spent the next few weeks thinking my dad was god as well. I realised if I still got my presents no matter how bad I was, I wouldn't get into trouble for sinning."

Warrick grinned. "Least I'm not the only one."

"So, if it really does end, what do you wish you had done differently?"

They sat silently, reflecting for a few moments.

Andrews spoke first. "I would have told people I loved them. You think they know. But I guess sometimes people need to be told."

The woman lit another joint. After a few puffs she held it out to warrick. He looked at it for a second or two, then without saying a word took a few drags.

"I guess I wouldn't have become a policeman."

Andrews looked at hi in surprise.

"I'm serious. I thought it was all about helping people. You know, they're the bad guys, we're the good guys. But it's not like that."

"So what would you have done?"

"I don't know. I quite fancied becoming one of those volunteers that travel the world, going to places that need help. What about you two?"

"I would have moved to Amsterdam and started my own weed farm. Pensioners and disabled people would get it half price. I would have had a little bar, with a little free foodstuff laid out. You know, Sunday pub food. Some roast potatoes, shellfish, maybe mackerel on toast."

The man looked at her. "You don't eat shellfish."
"I wouldn't be eating it. I'd be too busy in testing the merchandise. Quality control is an important part of any business venture."
She picked up the popcorn, opened the bag and offered it around.
"Cheers," said Andrews, taking a large handful. "What about you mate?"
"Not sure. I suppose I should be. Regrets and all that. But if I changed those things, would I be me? I guess I wish I was less scared to make decisions. I always think what if it goes wrong, so I don't do anything."
"Are you two married?"
The man and woman grinned at each other.
"No chance. Just mates. Have been for longer than I can remember. But we don't see each other much."
"But you chose to spend this time with each other. What about your families or loved ones?"
"I don't date. He dates all the time. I don't think either of us are cut out for it."
"What about you two?"
"Andrews is married to the job." He dodged a playful punch from his partner. "I've been seeing this girl. I suppose it's serious. I've never really thought about it."
Ask yourself, if this is it, you'll never see her again. How would you feel?"
"Don't say that."
"It's true though," said Andrews solemnly. "I guess that's how you know it's love. You can't imagine a time without them."
Warrick shifted uncomfortably. "I s'pose."
"What you said before, about them being the bad guys and you being the good, what did you mean?"
"Well, it's people. Sometimes you can't work out who is the victim and who is the perpetrator. It's ok when

you know. But there's people who fit into the wrong section. Society looks at them as the bad guy, we know they're a victim. Vice versa. It should be like the cowboy films, bad guys wear a black hat, good guys wear white."

"He's right," nodded andrews. "You get some bloke demanding you nick some kid pinching from his shop. But you just know the bloke beats his wife, you just can't prove it. And the kid he wants you to arrest probably hasn't had a decent meal in weeks. It's all wrong."

"It would be a great job if you could know and prove who the bad guy was. But even then they change from day to day."

"Is that why you want to quit?"

"I never said I wanted to quit, just that I don't think I would have started."

"But if you know you're not happy and know what you would rather do, then why stay?"

"I guess coz now I'm in it with them."

The man frowned. "What do you mean?"

"Well it's like any job. You get your regulars. I don't just mean the crims or the drunks, but people on your beat. The old lady who comes in about losing her bag, even though she's just left it at home. Or the kids who look on you as their copper."

Andrews nodded. "And the ordinary people. They just want to get through each day as normal as possible. They turn to you about the vandals and burglars. They look to you to sort it."

"That's right. It's the good guys against the rubbish. They see us as the good guys. To abandon the job would feel like abandoning them."

"But there will be other policemen. Someone would replace you."

Andrews and warrick exchanged a glance.

"Not all coppers are nice people. We know we're not perfect, but we're better than some."

"Fair enough."

"How long?"

The man looked at his watch. "Twenty five minutes."

"So how's it supposed to happen? World explodes? Meteor?"

Andrews answered. "The centre of the world reaches critical, causing an internal explosion which cracks the planets surface beyond repair. Volcanoes and earthquakes erupt everywhere but we get poisoned by all the escaping gasses."

The man grinned. "You know a lot for a sceptic."

Andrews laughed. "I'm mainly into the conspiracy theories regarding off world visitors and their technologies. According to Jacs Facts, all the aliens know about our impending doom, that's why they've been abducting us over the years."

"Ah, but according to Wookies Word, they're the ones who cause the planets core to go critical. Some of their advanced technology."

Warrick looked at his partner. "You never told me about all this."

Andrews raised an eyebrow. "The truth is out there."

"It's just finding it in all the junk."

"So what else haven't you told me? On your day off do you go UFO hunting."

"I may have done once or twice."

"See anything?"

"Not that I would discuss with a non believer."

"Oh come on, how are you supposed to convince us sane people if you don't share?"

"I rest my case."

"What?"

Andrews remained silent.

The woman laughed. "I think it was the words sane people that did it."

The man looked at his watch. "Ten minutes and counting guys."

There was silence for a moment.

"Do you think there is a god?"

"Yeah, my dad."

"No, I mean really."

"Well we might find out in ten minutes."

"Yeah, but I mean, shouldn't be thinking about those regrets? The sins we've committed."

"I'm not sure I feel comfortable hearing that from a policeman. What sins?"

"I don't know, coveting, stealing, that sort of thing."

"You've stolen?"

"When I was a kid. We've all done it."

"Not me."

"I haven't."

"You're on your own mate."

They laughed at warricks expression.

"Seriously," said the woman. "If there is a god, like the big policeman in the sky, he wouldn't care about the little things like that. He'd be more interested about people who go around torturing and killing. Didn't do that when you were a kid as well did you?"

"Ha ha, very funny."

The dog raised its head and whined.

The people became silent and looked out the window apprehensively.

The dog laid its head back on Andrews knee. Suddenly the car was filled with a noxious smell.

The man opened the window wider. "Sorry. It's the burgers."

All four tried to wave the smell out of the car. The dog licked its lips contentedly and settle back to sleep.
"Jesus, would we even notice the poisonous gasses."
"Three minutes."
"God, I didn't realise I would be this nervous."
"You sure that was the dog just now?"
The woman lit up her final joint. "Well this is it guys. Either no tomorrow or off to the cop shop."
"Do you think that'll be some sort of warning? Like a loud noise and hissing, or will we just fall unconscious?"
"I'd expect at least a rumble. Something. It would be a bit sad, just nothingness."
The woman passed warrick the joint. He hastily took a few puffs before handing it back.
"I s'pose I should hope it is the end. If they do a random drug test, I'll be stuffed anyway."
"Should we put the radio on? I mean, they'd be the first to know."
"Did you particularly want to hear a bunch of people you don't know screaming and choking to death?"
"Putting it like that, no, not really."
The man flipped on the radio. The car was filled with the sound of John Lennon gently asking people to imagine.
The four people in the cruiser sat back, closed their eyes and waited for oblivion.

Childish Thoughts

Last week I didn't want to eat my vegetables and my dinner lady said children in Africa were starving and I should be grateful for the food I got. When I got home I watched the news and I saw that the dinner lady was right and there was children starving. They were so hungry they had turned into stick people. The man said if they got no food soon they would die. I asked my dad can we send our vegetables to the children in Africa and he said don't be silly.

The next day my teacher told us about the desert and how it never rains and no plants can grow. She said people lost in the desert might never be found it was so big and they would die of thirst. When I got home I watched the news and the woman said that too much rain had fallen in one country and if it didn't stop soon the people would be flooded, their crops ruined and disease would come because of all the water and the people would die. I asked my dad why everyone didn't fill up a bucket with the water and take it to the desert so that the plants could grow and the people that were lost would not die of thirst and he said what a question.

On Saturday my brother took me to the river. We skipped stones and tried to catch fish with our hands. My brother told me all about the rats that live in the sewer and riverbanks. He said thousands and thousands come out at night and swim up through your toilet. He said that if a whole load of them were stuck in a room with you they might eat you to death but mostly they were harmless. He said that in poor countries the people ate rats but we don't because we have cows and sheep, which are a lot bigger so we don't need to eat them. That night I asked my dad why we couldn't catch the rats in our toilet and send them to poor countries for their dinner and he said he didn't know where I got my ideas from.

So yesterday on my way to the shops with my dad I asked him why can't we send the food we don't like to Africa and the rats to poor countries and the rain to the desert and he said I would understand when I was bigger and older. But I asked my brother who was bigger and he didn't know. So I asked my granddad who is very old and he didn't know either so I wonder if I'll ever be big enough or old enough to understand why we don't help stop all the people from dying.

Therapy

DC Jamison looked up at the building with some trepidation.
She was still unsure why her boss had sent her here. He had told her to make an appointment to visit Dr Naraja at the Neptune Mental Health Clinic. She had asked which case it referred to, doubting the answer to be either of the cases she was working on at the moment. He had said it was unrelated to any specific case, but that she would find it invaluable information. He had refused to say more.
Intrigued, she had contacted the doctor and been told to report at the clinic at nine o'clock this morning.
Jamison had always disliked hospitals in general, but mental health places especially gave her the willies. Crazies were something she had feared as a child, ever since Handbag Hetty who had lived in the park, shouted and screamed abuse at her.
The old lady shouted at everyone, but Jamison was sure the woman hated her and would find out where she lived. She stayed away from the park for two years because of it. And now, still, she tended to avoid the homeless or beggars, just in case they turned out to be Handbag Hetty.
Shivering a little, she entered the modern clinic and made her way to reception.
A small woman in a flowery dress was waiting for her.
"Good Morning, you must be DC Jamison, I'm Dr Naraja. Please come up to my office."
"Thank you."
Once upstairs, the doctor led the way into a small office and sat down behind the desk.

Jamison gave an embarrassed smile. "I was told to come here and see you by my superior, Inspector Rickman.."

"That's right. I've known Robert many years. Occasionally I let one of his favoured students sit a session or two."

"Favoured?" she couldn't help herself.

Dr Naraja smiled. "Yes. He thinks you'll go far. He's one of the most astute judges of character I've met. He thinks you are worth training."

"He doesn't say much."

"No. If you're good at your job, you know what needs doing. He knows you can do it, so he lets you."

"Um… I'm not really sure…"

"Yes, I know. You don't know why Robert asked you to see me. In a moment, I'm going to take you to an observation room, over-looking one of my sessions. It's a group session. You will be watching them, listening to what they say. After the session, we will discuss what you have learned. I can't really answer any questions yet, but I think you will benefit from what you learn."

"Ok, I guess. Am I allowed to observe? I mean, won't they mind?"

"The group know that the sessions are being recorded and they know that occasionally there are observers. They don't really think about it. But obviously it would be different if you were in the room. They would not talk freely then."

"No, I can understand. Ok. Well, ready when you are."

The doctor smiled. "I can see why Robert sent you, you are willing to learn, so many people are not. Ok let's go."

After settling Jamison in the observation room, Dr Naraja went in to the connecting room and sat down on a small chair.

The group sat in a circle. A few were tearful, all were silent. The session was obviously not the first with this group and Dr Naraja greeted them all easily.

"Ok, I want us to pick up where we left off last time. Now, Greg," she turned to a small man, sitting hunched up in his seat. "Your friend was suffering, in constant pain, did he attempt suicide more than once?"

"Yes. I didn't know. But he told me. He said he couldn't do it. he would try, but it just didn't work. He kept saying, help me Greg, you gotta help me."

At that moment Greg's voice broke off and he lowered his head. The tears began rolling down his cheeks.

"That's ok Greg, we'll leave it there for now. Ok, let's move on. Cole? Had there been any previous attempts?"

The large man sitting in the chair opposite Dr Naraja nodded.

"For the first year of Tammy's death, there were three over-doses. She also tried cutting her wrists and..uh…hanging herself. But none of it worked. Each time she seemed further and further away from emotion, reality. And then she just gave up. She seemed to except life, living, but not in a healthy way. It was like she was just sitting there, waiting for it to end." Cole's eyes filled and he turned them upwards in an effort to keep the tears back. "Then she seemed to come out of it. She started doing housework, looking at the bills, all the things she did before. I really thought she was better."

It sounded like a plea, begging them to understand.

"I really did." He paused, swallowed then continued. "When I got up she was spring cleaning the kitchen, you know, defrosting the fridge and degreasing the oven. I was just thankful that she was doing something so normal, something sane. And I went to work."

The large man to a big painful breath and let it out in a heavy sigh. He clenched his fists, forcing his voice to be steady he went on.

"I came home and the house was so quiet, so still. I thought she was out, but then I saw the coat on the banister. I think that's when I knew. I called out, panicking. I rushed upstairs, dreading I would find her with blood all over her or hanging somewhere. But she was nowhere to be found. I went out to the kitchen to see if she had left a note. I didn't see it at first. I put the kettle on, got my cup ready, wondering if she had popped over to a neighbours. Then…then I went to get the milk. That's when I saw the note on the fridge. It said 'I love you. Don't open the fridge. Call the police.' I just sat down, knowing, but saying it was impossible. I must be wrong, oh please god let me be wrong, but I had to know. I had to do it. I had to open it. She was there, and her face…oh god."

Cole shuddered. He covered his face as if trying to block out the picture. Then his hands lowered.

"I called an ambulance. I don't know why, she had been dead for hours, but it was all I could think to do. While I was waiting I held her and talked to her. And then I started laughing. I know how it sounds, but I had realised she defrosted the fridge because she didn't want to be cold. And that's what she was like. She had the stupidest, smartest logic. It always made a weird sense." He smiled. Then his face sobered. "The police and ambulance arrived. They took me to the hospital as well, said I was suffering from shock. And maybe I was. I kept laughing and crying, but none of it seemed really real."

He coughed, straightened himself up. "That was three years ago. I can't go out much. I don't go to friends houses. I don't invite them over. I can't watch T.V. Because I still can't look at a refrigerator and they're everywhere. Whenever I do I feel sick. Everything goes too bright and starts spinning, I become hysterical if someone opens one in front of me. I know it's a rational fear, considering the circumstances, but knowing doesn't stop it. And the worst thing is sometimes I hate her. I wish she'd jumped out of a window or off a cliff.. And I shouldn't wish that, should I? I should wish she was still alive." Cole closed his eyes and lowered his head.

"*Do* you wish she was still alive?" The doctor asked kindly.

Cole opened his eyes and looked at her. "No."

"Why not?"

"Because I spent three years waiting for her to die. Every day, coming home and waiting to find her either dead or dying, everyday waiting for a phone call. When she succeeded, it was like the waiting was over for both of us. But this part is not how I thought it would be, and I keep thinking, if it wasn't for the fridge, would it be?"

"You mean the grieving?"

Cole nodded. "She died when Tammy died. But I couldn't grieve for both of them and she was still by my side in body. Tammy was gone, but we both existed. Maybe if she had succeeded the first time, I would have been ok. But I held on to that grief, pretended she would pull through it. But after the second attempt, I knew it was only a matter of time. Even when I thought she was getting better, I guess deep down inside, I knew it wasn't over yet."

"Do you think you would still have been angry with her if she had succeeded the first time?"
Cole nods slowly. "Because she left me. When our daughter had died and I needed her most, she left me." He tapped his head. "In there, I was alone. I had to keep the house together, see to the arrangements, pay the bills and be the strong one. And mostly I could do it, but there were times I needed to let go, and I wasn't able. I hurt so bad and she was gone from me. The one person who had been with me through everything. The one person I shared my soul with. I needed to hold her and be held by her, but there was just this shell. And I was alone."
"Ok group. Tom, do you have any thoughts?"
"Yes. I…I think that the fridge has become a way," he swallowed. "A way of avoiding your wife."
The woman in the flower dress looked at him. "Go on."
"You… you never mention your wife's name. Because of your fear of fridges, you can use it as an excuse not to see your friends, but really it's because they might say her name."
A thin faced woman sat forward, nodding. "It becomes a cycle. You don't want anything that reminds you, so you don't watch TV in case her favourite programme comes on. You don't go out in case you meet someone who knew her, or looks like her. I bet you don't shop in the same places you used too."
Cole looks at them. "You're wrong."
Greg spoke. "But you said your daughters name. Tammy. You said it several times. Obviously her death, in some way, was an acceptable death. It's ok to say Tammy's name."
"I've accepted my wife's death."

A teenage girl sat forward and shook her head. "No, you accepted that it would happen, but not why. Because in a time of need, she didn't turn to you, she turned to oblivion. Are you angry because you think she loved Tammy more than you?"

"How dare you."

"I'm not saying it's true. I'm asking is that how you feel?"

Dr Naraja looked at her. "Is that how you feel Tessa?" The young woman looked at the therapist.

"I did, at first. I was nine when my momma died of cancer. When we found out she had it, she only had a couple of months left. Two weeks after the funeral, my father shot himself. I decided my mother must have got cancer on purpose and that she and my dad planned it. So they could go and live together in heaven without me. Because they never took me with them. They didn't want me, didn't love me the way they loved each other."

"What changed your mind?" asked Greg curiously.

Tessa gave a twisted smile. "When I was twelve, I had a friend named Cathy. Her family were catholic. When I told her what I thought, she said 'Oh no. Your father committed suicide, he won't get into heaven.'" Tessa looked down at her hands, then back at the group. "I asked her what she meant and she told me all about religion and the different rules. I was really confused then, because it meant that my father hadn't wanted to be in heaven with my mother and he would rather go to hell than stay on earth with me."

"How do you feel now?"

"I don't...I've never... I understand that pain, emotional or physical, can be so bad you can't take anymore, but I've never felt it. I've seen it, in other people, but I've never felt it about anyone or anything.

But I don't believe in heaven or hell now, I just know my parents no longer exist. But I don't feel happy or sad about it. It just is."

The thin faced woman sat forward but the therapist held up her hand to silence her.

"What about other aspects in your life, Tessa?" she asked. "Is there sadness or happiness there?"

"Not really, I get up, go to work, come home, sleep, get up. There's not much to be happy or sad about. It's just life."

"Group. What do you think Cole?"

"I have nothing to say."

"Why not?"

"I don't know."

"Ok. Greg?"

"I think that a lack of emotion can be as damaging and problematic as too much. There should be some kind of balance. That's why we are here. People we knew or loved felt too much or not enough. I think that deep inside you there is someone still feeling. But you've numbed yourself to it. The pain can't touch you, but neither can the joy. Cole was waiting for his wife to die. I think you are waiting to die. You won't take your own life, but you are just waiting for your existence to be over."

"Aren't we all, one way or another?"

The thin-faced woman shook her head vehemently. "No. We make our pain and we make our pleasure. We have to seek out the joy, else we become like them and wallow in the pain. That's why they killed themselves, because they allowed themselves to wallow in pain. If they had done something positive, they would have felt something. But they didn't." Her voice became bitter. "They shut themselves away until they couldn't take it anymore."

Tom stared at her. "How can you say that Clair? Don't you know what it's like for people? I can understand people committing suicide over love of someone. What I can't understand is people being driven to it, seeing no other way out. That is something I will never understand."

"It's a choice," Clair sniffed dismissively.

"Not always. Do you know what it's like for a child, to be bullied day after day? And I don't mean just taking your dinner money. I mean making your life a living hell. Day after day, beatings, humiliations and no matter what you do, it never stops. That no one listens to you. No one helps you. Your twelve years old and alone. And the only way to stop it is to jump from a building. Twelve years old. We didn't know, not all of it, not till after, but we should have listened. Should have taken it seriously."

"I still say it was a choice. He could have run away or called the authorities."

"He came to me. I'm his uncle. He trusted me. But I was busy, I wasn't really listening. He said there was a bully at school. I told him a bully must be stood up to. It was time for him to be a man. I told him not to pick a fight, but just learn to defend himself, stand up for himself. Then I left." Tom shook his head. "He came to me, and I drove him to it as much as the bullies. There were five of them, not one. When he tried to 'defend himself', they made his life a worse misery. And he felt he wasn't a man, because he couldn't stand up to them. I made my nephew feel like he wasn't a man coz he couldn't fight five boys twice the size of him."

"But you didn't know there were five."

"Because I never stopped to listen. I should have asked him about it, not assumed it was rough house for pecking order. What those boys did was out and out evil. They were expelled. Expelled! They should have gone to prison for life."

"But if he'd gone to the authorities..." Clair persisted.

"Don't you listen? If I had told him that in the first place he would be alive now. That's what I mean about driven. They made him want to die, I gave him no way out."

"I agree with you," said Cole. "About the bullies I mean. I mean it was a form of murder."

"No." said Clair firmly. "It wasn't. Suicide is suicide. For whatever reason, that person no longer wants to exist and so ends their life."

"But you can't lump it all together," argued Greg.

"But it is," she insisted.

"No. I agree there is a choice element, but a boy jumping because he lives in constant torment is different than someone who has a terrible disease and is in constant pain. The person with the disease chooses to end his life now. The child was driven and could have been saved, should never have had to live that life."

"They were both in pain and decided to end it the same way. There is no difference, it's suicide."

"But an adult who is in constant pain should be allowed to make that choice, a child should never want to."

"But if you are going to hell for suicide, won't the torment and pain that is faced there be more than is faced here."

Tessa looked at Clair but said nothing.

Greg answered. "That only works if you believe in the whole God and Heaven stuff."

"But I do. And that's I can't understand why people would chose it. People that have been God fearing all their lives. People that understand what the sanctity of life really means, committing that sin. That I don't understand. What does it achieve? Knowing you are going to go somewhere far worse, what does it achieve?"

Tessa stared fixedly at Clair, still saying nothing. She was sitting up straighter than she had throughout the session.

Again it was Greg that spoke. "Perhaps they can't imagine anyplace worse than where they are."

"But it is, infinitely so."

"But like I said that only works if you believe in God."

"And I do. Which is why I know all the people you knew will be in hell."

Tessa began shifting in her seat. The therapist glanced at her, but the girl seemed intent only on the conversation.

Clair continued. "And it makes me so angry. God is there, here, all around, all you need do is turn to him. But instead they turn their backs and fall into Hell."

Tessa shot her a malicious look. "So, like you said, if he knew all this, why did he? I mean really?"

"Guilt," Clair answered in disgust. "Which is foolish. All you need is ask for Gods forgiveness. He had a sinful soul, we all have, we are born to it. But knowing that it is wrong, we strive to repel those thoughts, for Satan is trying to tempt and turn us. Instead of fighting those temptations, he gave into them. And when I confronted him with it, told him he must give himself up, he decided to take his life. He turned completely from God."

Tessa met her gaze. "There is no God."

"You are wrong."

Tessa continued to look at Clair. The other's became a little uncomfortable.

Dr Naraja smiled. "Ok group. Well that's it for now, see you for the next session tomorrow."

After leaving the room, Dr Naraja went to collect Jamison, before going back to her office for coffee. She poured two mugs, passed one to Jamison and then went to sit behind her desk.

Jamison accepted the coffee gratefully, she felt drained. "Thanks, look, I don't really understand. I mean, no offence, but suicide doesn't come under criminal offence. Not anymore."

"What did you think of the people you met?"

"Individually, or as a group?"

"Both. Group first."

"Pity."

"Why?"

"Because they were all living with the aftermath of something they didn't create. I know they all feel some responsibility for the deaths, because they are all still affected by it."

"Do you think they are responsible?"

"No, definitely not. I mean, perhaps some of them could have done things different, but even then, there's nothing to say it would have worked."

"What do you think of them individually?"

"Cole I felt the most sorry for. I mean I don't think I could ever open a fridge again either, and because he lost both his wife and his daughter."

"You think his grief was the greater?"

"No. I think that's Tessa. I mean a child losing her mother and father in such a traumatic way. And I think she is grieving what she sees as a lack of their love, as well as their death. Even though she no longer responds to emotion."

"What about Tom?"

"Tom is complex. I feel pity, but I also feel anger. Why didn't he listen. The boy's suicide, out of all of them, should have been avoidable."

"What about Greg?"

"Well Greg and Clair I don't feel pity for, but for different reasons. Greg, I don't know why he's here. He seems pretty balanced and he understand the reason the person in his life committed suicide."

"Clair?"

"Clair? I don't know...she frightens me. I don't know why. I guess because she shows the most anger about it, although I suppose that's pretty normal. But she feels no compassion or pity. Only that...arrogance that people could be so stupid. So I don't know why she's here either."

Dr Naraja lent back in her chair.

"I am, of course, prevented from telling you all details, but lets just say that the suicides they talked about has completely altered their lives."

"Ok."

"So what if I were tell you that two of those suicides were not. They were murder."

Jamison sat up. "What? But...which ones?"

The therapist laughed. "You're the trainee detective, can't you tell?"

"Well, I guess I wasn't looking at them like that. After Cole's story, I just sort of assumed..."

"I know. Very horrific detail, puts you in one frame of mind. It may have been unfair to lead with him. But I didn't want you to look at them as suspects, but as people, humans."

"I guess. But know I'm confused. Now I'm trying to slot them in as murderers."

"And?"

"And I want it to be Clair."

"Well at least that's honest. Because you feel no pity for her?"

"No, because it hasn't affected her. Not in the way it has affected Cole and Tom, or even Tessa. I suppose I'd say the same of Greg." New frowned. "But then Tessa is the most repressed. She showed little emotion. Cole? Perhaps he did put his wife in the fridge, which is why he can't face them or say her name."

"Tom?"

"I can't see a reason for Tom to push his nephew off a building, unless he were the bully. But I can't see that because the fury he felt was real."

"Ok, so who do you think is most likely?"

Jamison let out a long breath. "I can't decide between Cole and Greg on one side and Tessa and Clair on the other. It's like they are both opposites of each other, passion and calm."

"So you still leave out Tom?"

"Yes. Like I said, how he felt about those bullies, and himself, I don't think he killed his nephew."

"Ok. Well, see you tomorrow for the next session."

"What? No, you have to tell me."

Dr Naraja smiled. "All will be revealed."

Jamison sat in the observation room, waiting for the next session to start.

All night she had been running through her mind which one could be the murderer. Or murderers. She still wanted it to be Clair, but she realised that was also a professional ego. She wanted to be able to pick out a killer through instinct. And maybe it would be vanity to say so, but she thought she could.

In the next room, Dr Naraja sat down and greeted the group.

"Ok, yesterday we were discussing the reasons that led you all here. Today we are going to discuss key points. You remember we talked about those before and what they mean. I want each of you to state your Key Moment. Remember, the answer should be short. Don't think about it too long. Ok?"

The group gave it's various assents.

"Cole, tell us about your Key Moment."

"It had been a bad week. I kept having the dreams; they wouldn't go away. Over and over my wife crying in the house, and I couldn't help her. I wanted so much to help her. I woke up, covered in sweat, so scared. There was someone knocking on the door. I opened it, and there was this man, a delivery man, with a fridge."

"Ok. Tom?"

"I don't know. It built up. I just knew it was the only way to stop the suffering, to stop *him* from suffering. It just built up until I couldn't see anything else."

"Greg?"

"He was crying. I'd never seen that before. Never in all the years we'd known each other."

"Clair?"

"When I saw the letter he had written. I'd admired him, his devotion, his worth and it was all a lie. That person I'd admired didn't really exist. He would rather go to Hell than ask for God's forgiveness. He was a priest for goodness sake."

"Tessa?"

"The words. Exactly the same words."

"Ok. Now Greg. You said your friend asked for help. Did you?"

Greg nodded. "The pills just made him sick and I didn't know what else to do. So I waited till he was asleep and I suffocated him with his pillow."

"Cole, what happened when you saw the delivery man?"

"I told him to take it away, but he wouldn't. I was screaming at him. She was in there. I know she was. I hit him again and again, over and over, till someone pulled me off. He died of massive head injuries."

"Tom, what happened that day?"

"They were standing there, bullying some kid, and I knew it was never going to end. My nephew was dead, but the torment would go on for some other kid. I had to stop it. Stop them. I got the jack out of the car and I killed them. Smashed every one of their heads in. They can't hurt anyone else again."

"Tessa, what did the woman say?"

"She was living in the block. Just one of those crazy religious women, always spouting stuff about the bible. She started going on about God's purpose, God's plan. I got so angry, I yelled at her, asking what purpose my mother's dying of cancer and my father blowing his brains out where. She looked at me with such pity, the same way my friend had, and said 'Your father is in Hell.' I hated her. I just struck out, telling her to shut her mouth, I smashed her head in." Tessa stared at Clair in a meaningful way, but the older woman did not seem to notice.

"Is that what you did to your friend Cathy?"

Tessa nodded. "People thought she'd fainted and fallen on a rock on the way home from school, but she didn't."

"Clair, what happened when you saw the letter?"

"It was so pathetic. He was crying. He hadn't expected me round, but I knew it had to be sorted out. I had come round to assure him I wasn't going to the police, but that he would have to confess to the bishop. When I got there, he was just about to hang himself. I read the letter and saw him for the weak, pitiful creature he was. However, I had been his friend for many years. I felt it my duty. When his back was turned, I secured a knife and killed him. I will be forgiven for sleighing him, as God forgives those who ask. And he died without committing the sin of suicide. My conscience is clear."

"I think we should break for now. "

Back in Dr Naraja's office, Jamison sat down and glared at the therapist.
"You cheated."
"No. The other cases were suicide, only Greg's and Clair's were murder. Robert wanted to show you that it's not always simple. None of those people would have killed, if suicide, or the want of, had not somehow touched their lives. That is what connects that group of people. If the people in their lives had not wanted to die, then with the exception of Clair, none of them would have killed."
"You said the exception of Clair."
"Yes. There are born killers and I think she is one of them. She feels only herself in situations. Pain of a child being bullied, tortured by dreams, fear that her father resides in hell and compassion for another human being. All reasons and all faced. But Clair lies about her reasons, self disgust of worshipping an unworthy idol. Because she felt in control of that while she thought she in control of him. He would repent, he would be saved. But he chose a different way out. That pushed her over the top, but I think she's the type anyway. If not him, another."
"I don't know how I feel, how I'm supposed to feel. I just still feel so sorry for most of them."

"Good. Just because somebody kills, doesn't mean they are a killer."

"I've always known that, but I guess I never really did."

"None of these people can be let out in society. Even though we may understand why they did it, even agree in the case of Tom and Greg, and know it's not their fault in the case of Tessa and, especially, Cole, but they cannot be let free because they killed and may do so again."

"It just seems so…sad."

"It is. And that's what Robert wanted you to learn. Finding out why someone kills is important, and so is stopping them, but sometimes you need to understand the person, and feel that compassion, because otherwise they just become numbers."

"Thank you for letting me sit in. It's given me a lot to think about."

Jamison left the building, but was unsure she would ever be able to leave the people behind.

Dr Naraja was right, at times, she had thought of the crimes committed and the people that committed them as just cases, numbers, but they were not, they were people, with complicated pasts and futures.

She would certainly look at suicide cases and murderers a lot differently now.

As she drove away, she took a last glimpse of the clinic. It was something that would never have occurred to her, that murderers would need therapy.

Food for Thought

The Queen Bea

On board a small salvage ship called the Queen Bea, the bridge crew looked out the observation portal at the supplies dock in front of them.
It was only a sub port but, as the next supply was four weeks away, it was a welcome sight.
Captain Monay, referred to by most of his crew as Cap, rubbed his eyes tiredly.
"Ok, scan it," he ordered.
"All showing green, Cap. Minimal Life, nothing more than a few mice, spiders and that's about it."
"But the cold, surely that would kill them?" asked Spinelli, the pilot.
"Always a few hardy bastards. Ok, Tanner, Crop, I want you two suited and booted. You're out in fifteen. I just want a look round before we party."
"Aye Cap."
The two men left the bridge.
"Ok, Spinelli, bring it to the dock area, but not too close. We need to be able to leg it before we have to."
"Aye Cap."
The captain flicked open an intercom.
"Ok boys and girls, we are on full alert. Once the dynamic duo give us the all clear, I want those available for retrieval. Dr Stace, I want them scanned constantly and I want an all clear before they're allowed back through the airlock."

"Yes Captain."
"Ok Spinelli, how goes?"
"Just lined up, the lads can go at any time."
Cap flipped a switched. "Ok, Tanner, you're on point. Off you go lads, tread careful."
"Aye Cap."

Stock Port H30321

Crop Davis, recon expert and Queen Bea's youngest crewmember, looked at his partner in crime.
"Two people and you're on point. We've not got guns, just a fire stick and ice pole. Daft is what it is. He thinks he's still in the bleedin' army."
"You want to go first?"
"Cap says you. Orders are orders. I'll stand right behind you."
"You would ya poof. You aint getting in this suit, so keep your eyes off me arse."
"You'd have to lose a few pounds; it's bigger than you are. How's any one supposed to see anything else sweetheart."
"You'll see my fist soon enough."
"You He-man you."
"Shut up and help me get this door open."
The two men entered the external airlock of the supply station. Tanner operated the decompression unit. Within a few moments, a light turned green and the inner door opened.
Tanner spoke into his mike. "Queen Bea, this is Cowboy One, do you read?"
"Cowboy One, this is Queen Bea, go ahead."
"Ok, we're in. Everything looks standard. Temps lower than I thought it would be, but that's about it.

We've searched the base floor, just heading up to the next level. There's only two and it's set out as open plan."
"Roger Cowboy One. Standing by."
Crop raised his eyebrows. "What do they think is going to happen? I mean, anything weird would have been picked up by the scanners, right?"
"It's just standard procedure; you know that, stop whining."
"Is that an order Mr 'On Point'?"
"Damn straight. While it's just us out here, your arse is mine."
"See, I knew you were begging for it. I'm irresistible to everyone."
"You wish."
"Did you see those crates of peaches? When was the last time you had a real peach?"
"Can't remember the last time I ate anything real. Been out here too long dude."
"Tell me about it."

The Queen Bea

Dr Stace, chief medico, was studying pictures of outside the station. He looked intently at the x-ray of the hull. Suddenly he lent forward in shock.
"Shit. Cap, we've got to go, now."
"What?"
"Look." Stace pointed to an enlargement of the picture. Six tiny, almost invisible, circular outlines could be seen at the bottom of the hull.

Cap turned to the scanner reader angrily. "You said it was clean, for god sake." He hit the intercom. "We're out of here, make ready. Spinelli, take us out."
"But Tanner and…"
"It's too late for them. Move."
Spinelli did as ordered. Soon the station was a distant spec.
"Space maggots," growled the captain as he stomped off the bridge.

Stock Port H30321

Crop followed his friend as he made his way over to the far wall, and began examining the stacks of crates and boxes.
Suddenly he lifted his head in puzzlement.
"Tanner?"
"What?"
"The ship just fired up."
Tanner stopped what he was doing. He frowned.
"Maybe they just got too close and had to move back."
"But they would have said something."
"Queen Bea, Queen Bea, this is Cowboy One, do you read?"
Silence.
"Queen Bea, this is Cowboy One, copy?"
"They've gone."
"Course they haven't. They wouldn't just abandon us. It might be my transmitter. Try yours."
"Queen Bea, this is Cowboy two, respond."
Silence.
"Respond you wankers."
Nothing.

"They've fucked off and left us."
"Don't be an idiot. Something must have happened. They'll be back."
"So what do we do now?"
"Well we won't starve, that's for sure. And there's oxygen enough. Let's bring some boxes round, make ourselves an area."
"Why?"
"Because it will be warmer than sitting in the open. Besides, if we do it near the lock, it'll take less time to load when they do return."
"You mean if."
"I mean when. They wouldn't just leave us, no word, nothing."
But inside Tanner felt a nagging doubt. The Cap wasted little o n words, and even less on sentiment, but if they *had* been abandoned, why? The scanners had picked up nothing. They themselves could find nothing wrong, and their own scanner equipment said there were no diseases here. Why had the Queen Bea fled, with no word of return?
Trying to keep himself too busy to ask questions, Tanner set out to gather boxes and began building a warmer area. Crop soon got involved and, within an hour, they had built themselves a fair den.
"I'm starving."
"You're always starving. Grab some of those peaches. There's some tinned ham here."
"Got a tin opener?"
"As always."
Crop picked out a handful of peaches and laid the fruits between them.
Tanner was just about to open the tin of ham with the opener he always kept on his utility belt. He saw Crop lift one of the peaches to his mouth. The other side of

the peach moved. Something pushed out from under the skin.

"DON'T EAT IT."

"For god's sake, don't shout. I'm right next to you."

Crop looked at the peach; he saw movement under the skin. He yelled and threw the peach to the floor.

The fruit shattered and several short white worms wriggled across the floor. They inched their way closer to Crop, who abruptly stood up and began to back away.

"What the Fuck?"

Tanner stood up and squished the writhing insects.

The remaining peaches Crop had left on the floor began to split open. Fifty white worms began wriggling towards the two men.

Crop began splatting them as fast as he could.

Tanner let out a cry and pointed to the stack of crates. The worms were crawling out between the slats in their hundreds. As they hit the floor, they began inching their way towards the two men. Tanner crashed his way out of the box made shelter and ran towards the stairs.

"This way, Crop, off the ground."

He climbed up, two at a time, his heavy breathing all but masking a dry yet slithery sound. As Crop appeared beside him, he looked down and saw what was causing the noise. Everywhere he looked; boxes were shedding thousands of small white bodies.

"Jesus fucking Christ, what the fuck is going on?"

"Space maggots."

Both men had heard stories about the creatures, but that's all it had been. Always tales told about them, but no one had ever seen them. No one Tanner had ever met, anyway. It was always this guy that knew someone who had worked with a guy whose brother had been on a ship with a guy whose uncle had seen them. No one really believed in space maggots.

"But it's just a story."

"Don't think so Crop. Not any more."

"But the scanners, why didn't they pick anything up?"

"Maybe they don't believe in them either. I don't know Crop."

"Bastards. They knew and they left us. Fucking bastards."

Tanner said nothing. What could he say? It was true. The captain had found out the place was infested and left them there. No one was coming back to rescue them. The Cowboys were on their own. Looking on the bright side, he and Crop had been mates for years, and he was glad the younger man was here. If you're going to get eaten alive, do it with friends. He felt a hysterical laugh forming and choked it off before it could erupt.

"They're climbing up the stairs Tanner."

He looked and saw Crop was right. It would take them time, but they would do it.

"Try the thrower."

The Queen Bea was not a military ship and besides, guns in space were a bad idea. Bullet holes in the wrong place could be more than just a problem; they could be death to the whole ship. But the captain had issued them with a flame thrower. Though a flame thrower was only a good weapon if you could put out the thing you had flamed, before it caught the surroundings and turned the whole place into an inferno. So they had been issued with an ice pole, a form of extinguisher. Both items were really a standard, in case they had encountered anything hostile. As far as Tanner could see, these maggots were incredibly hostile.

Crop, who had forgotten the throwers existence, swallowed dryly.

"I aint got it," he mumbled.

"What?"

"I said I aint got it. It's down there. I took it off when you started humping boxes."

"For Christ sake."

"You said it was clear, how was I supposed to know."

"So now what do we do?"

"Well, you've got the extinguisher, see if that helps"

Tanner, unlike Crop, had picked up the gun like equipment automatically, as he had run from the confines of the den. He slipped it from his shoulder, pointed it at the advancing mass and pulled the trigger in a short burst.

Once the mist had cleared, they could see the worms on the highest step had stopped their advance. They lay crackling slightly. Without pause, the lower ranks climbed over them and continued their ascent. A few slowed, caught by the coldness of the steps, but soon a layer of maggots was making its way up the next step.

"Do it again."

"No, there's no point, we can't waste it."

Tanner looked over the side of the staircase and onto the ground below. It was no a carpet of maggots, writhing, inching, their way to the stairs.

"Well do something then, they're on the fourth step."

Tanner looked around wildly. There was nowhere else to go. He looked up. A large hook on a chain, used for manoeuvring large crates, hung about three feet from the ceiling.

"Come on," he said and began stacking boxes underneath.

Crop, unsure of his intent, bent to help.

"Ok, up."

Crop climbed to the top and Tanner quickly joined him.
"Now what?"

Without saying a word, Tanner ran a length of wire several times around Crops arm. He then pulled the wire tight to the hook. Fumbling a little, he tried to do the same with his own. Crop, still not understanding, helped as best as he could.

"They're nearly at the top, Tan."

Tanner looked. As he did, a worm came into view over the top step. Followed by another, then three, six, a dozen. Tanner took a deep breath and then kicked away the boxes. Now they were dangling freely. The maggots couldn't reach them.

For a moment, he wondered if the would stand o each other to reach them, like some weird circus act, but he relaxed a little when he saw they couldn't.

"We can't just hang here forever, Tan. My arm already aches."

"We've got no choice Crop. Besides, maybe we don't have to."

He lowered the nozzle on the extinguisher ands sent a jet of cold liquid onto the mass below. As before, the wriggling stopped and slight crackling sounds could be heard. Immediately more maggots covered this layer and Tanner knew it wouldn't work. The extinguisher didn't hold that much, not enough for the teeming ass directly underneath and on the stairs, let alone for the white carpet below.

"Tan," Crop's voice sounded strange, almost childlike. "Tan, they're climbing the walls."

The Queen Bea

Dr Stace pulled roughly at the captain's arm.
"You can't just leave them there like that."
"They're dead already."
"Not them, the maggots. You have to destroy them. Don't you understand, if they get onto a passing ship, they'll be everywhere."
"They almost got onto ours."
"You have to go back."
"WHAT?"
"You have to go back and destroy that station."
"I don't have to do anything," the captain snapped, but he knew Stace was right, if anyone else stopped there…
He went back to the bridge.
The scanner was still sitting tearfully by her console. Spinelli looked at the captain. "How come the hull wasn't breeched, Cap?" If those things can eat through anything, then they should have breeched the stations integrity."
It was Stace that responded.
"These maggots aren't like normal maggots. They seal their entry points, so they can consume the insides without fear of being eaten by predators, or removed by their prey. These things don't just eat dead stuff; they eat anything they come into contact with. And, so long as they have some form of container, they can survive, even out there."
"So what do we do?"
Cap sat down in his seat. "We're going back and we're going to destroy that place, before they have a chance to destroy anything else."
Dr Stace walked over to the young scanner and tried to offer her some comfort. It wasn't her fault, he knew. The faint lines were almost invisible.

Monay sighed heavily. "Alright, bring her around. Load canister seven. Ready to fire?"
"Aye Cap."
As the ship came into view of the station, the captain hit the intercom. "Ok, I want her fired into the centre of that thing and I want us out on the wind. Got that?"
"Aye Cap."
"Aye Cap."
"Fire." Monay looked once more at the station. "Bye lads."

Stock Port H30321

In the station, the floor of maggots was starting to show gaps. Several lines of maggots moved up the wall and onto the ceiling. There they joined the mass that were hanging from the large hook, completely encompassing what little remained of Tanner and Crop.
A hole blasted into the wall and a canister flew across the room. For several seconds nothing, and then it exploded. Splinters of fire touched every surface and soon the station was nothing but a burnt out shell. Most of the maggots frizzled and fried in the intense heat and the sound of popping was a roar.
As the canister had entered, it had created a vacuum which had tried to suck everything out. In the event, two things managed to escape the inferno, a large box of tinned biscuits and a crate of peaches

The Friend

It was just a job.
If I had known it would all end in murder, I'm not sure I would have taken it.
I really don't think that just anyone could do my job; I think it has to be part of your genetic make up.
Lots of people are born that way, with an ability to put people at their ease, to subliminally instil an urge to unload, to share thoughts and dreams, to make people feel safe. It's a form of empathy, not only to listen to their problems or feelings, but have an understanding. Those born with the gift turn their talents to many professions; mediums, policemen, con artists, priests, therapists, even politicians and bar staff. I chose to be a professional friend.
I don't mean I'm employed by the people themselves to be their best buddy. I'm employed by their relevant interested parties to befriend certain people.
It's my job to be their confidante, advisor and babysitter without their knowledge that I'm being paid for those services. I'm there to make sure they meet the right people and avoid the wrong ones, to advise them against hasty choices and to subtly promote the ideas of my employers.
Usually I deal with actors, those in the music industry, relatives of royalty or eminent politician's offspring. I am never employed by the press or the general media, more agents, companies or official aides. I bring groups together or split them apart, but always without malice or violence.

There are professional trouble makers. Their job is to instil feelings of rage or distrust. To make sure an alky has plenty to drink, that indiscreet words are shouted around and blown out of proportion.

I am not that, nor ever would be. I am there to prevent problems before they happen.

I move about from lots of registered jobs, mostly as receptionist or PA to someone in hospitality. This means I have an official life as a temp and no one suspects my real employment. I am able to flit about with my 'friends' as needed, regardless of where they go.

Depending on the job, some are fleeting acquaintances, such as those that are one or two hit wonders, some are cultivated over years. Not only depending on how complex the direction I have to move them, but also how trusting they are.

And it doesn't do to alienate anyone who may go quiet on the scene, because you don't know when the might rise again in importance.

And even though I travel about, I must maintain my place on the edge of the scene, so that I am an always familiar, but never objected to, figure.

Do I tell my employers everything that is confided to me? Certainly not. If one of my charges had a romance with the boy next door at twelve, that's not my employers concern, unless there was a love child or blackmail involved.

I am not a spy; I am a safety net for my employer an unknowing client. No unexpected bombshells from the past or future. And, until that one job, I was bloody good at it.

You see, it's not a case of encouraging confession or relaxation while they are in a state of drug or alcohol induced intoxication. That just leaves people embarrassed and spending their time avoiding you. It should never be bullied or pried out. It should be given willingly, freely to someone who understands, and almost knows what you are about to say. Someone you just feel connected to, that you can talk or just be silent with. And that's where the main part of my talent comes in.

You see I study humans. I can't help it, I always have. I watch what they do and say in front of lots of different people. I collect, yet never share, gossip. And I listen, completely, to people when they are talking to me, without is distracting my attention from what's going on around me.

It's not just that I know who's sleeping, fighting, crying over, covertly watching who, but I know why.

I knew who were the trouble makers, who were the angels, who's voices spread which peoples words, and for what reasons.

I knew what people blinded themselves to be and their stark truths. Weakness, fears, hopes and aspirations, I knew them all. Because they told me, willingly, in shyness, in pride, in sorrow and without fear of them being used as weapons.

You may wonder how people like me find jobs. Obviously we can't advertise what we do. Mainly it's a job you fall into, then it spreads by word of mouth. People that need the use of those talents learn to recognise them in people, even though they don't possess those skills themselves (or perhaps because of it).

I don't always need to have any contact with my employers, other than a written form of instruction. I'm then paid as an employee in the area most likely to meet the unknowing client, be it at their beauty salon, library, night club, studio or with a friend of a friend.

It's all done very casually, yet with every intention of becoming a small part of that person's life. You would not guess that I already know everything that's said about you publicly and privately. You won't know that all my friends and acquaintances are unknowing clients like you. Either mine or someone else in the field. Because yes, we can recognise each other too.

But as to our actual employers, we might not even know who signs the checks if it's done through a trust fund. I know a couple of PF's that paints oil picture and write poems. Their work is hyped up so no one questions their bank balance.

The employer for this particular job was the Cigar Man. Please understand that in light of what happened I cannot use names, and at that time, I didn't even know his. I called him the cigar man because in the initial form of contract and instructions, and all further paperwork, lingering smell of cigar. It was a strong brand, though I was not really able to name it.

You must understand that I don't accept all jobs I'm offered, for several reasons. The first is that I can only be in so many places. I would soon be exhausted if I befriended all potential unknowing clients. Second, certain companies, i.e. press, criminal investigation and insurance companies, I refuse to work for. Or three, because something in the instructions doesn't sound right.

As I said, people like me are born this way, we don't choose it, we are naturally empathic, we can learn to enhance it or repress it, but we can never truly turn it off. I have spent years enhancing mine to the point that I get emanations from would be employers feelings and motivations.

Looking back, everything about that case was different, but I didn't see why. Just that everything that was being said was true. But there was something, an underlying excitement, and a coincidence.
Or so I thought.

A company I often worked for had asked me to befriend, some four years ago, a person I shall refer to as haunting voice. This was a one hit wonder singer/songwriter who had bought the nation to tears one Christmas, yet all three subsequent singles flopped and they were not heard from again in the main public. They drifted of the scene and into obscurity two years after their last release. From what I had heard, they had gone back to their former job in the hotel business.
I was informed by Cigar Man that in five years time HV would be ready to make a major comeback publicly. Up to that time, Cigar Man would be making sure that HV would be working on writing and recording material. My job was to make sure they kept out of trouble, had someone to talk to, and would pay for their taxi home at the end of the night if it came to it.
When the company had originally hired me to befriend HV, it was on a constant basis.
I cover three basics; constant, intermittent and on call. Most start in the first category, I may not be around them constantly, but I'm spending time evolving my life to suit theirs.
Intermittent is usually the second stage. They might not need my services for a while, or they might not welcome more than a casual, spontaneous, unplanned friendship.
On call can mean either, depending on how close the friendship has become or how much time has passed.

If they have moved to another country then another PF is enlisted and my role becomes obsolete or on hold. I find it pays to always retain some form of friendly feeling with most unknowing clients. They themselves can be a font of knowledge on a possible future client. And who knows, perhaps I also enjoy their companionship.

That company had basically dropped all befriending on HV two years ago. I had maintained the sending of Christmas cards and the occasional phone call, but mostly because I had never understood why Haunting Voice had been a one hit wonder.

I too had felt something had been missing from subsequent tracks, but was unsure as to what. I'd always had the hunch that HV would be heard from again.

When I got the contract from Cigar Man, I feel now that I was so smug that I had been right, that I paid more attention to the fact of who the unknowing client was, than who the possible employer might be.

From the empathic side, Cigar Man had total faith in HV. A seeming knowledge that HV was going to be a major, and I mean *Major*, star. The Cigar Man would move heaven and earth to make sure HV reached their full potential, and as far as he was concerned, it would be bigger than any of us could conceive. The belief just poured of the paper. Money was no object. Cigar man wasn't in it for the cash, he was in it because he wanted everyone on the planet to understand how intense and reaching HV really was.

Those are the reasons I accepted the job. How much hindsight shows us.

But there was something. That undercurrent of excitement had an element of something I didn't understand. It was even stronger when I actually found out who the Cigar Man was.

It happened by chance, most of my faceless employers I wouldn't know in a line up, but one night, while sitting in a restaurant, two people walked passed and instantly I recognised the smell. Cigar Man. It wasn't just the tobacco smell; it was that same underlying smell, when the smoke combines with the smell of shampoo, cologne, clean sweat. The smell of a person, unique as a fingerprint.

Without seeming to, I took note of his face when the opportunity presented. Although I didn't recognise him, it was now easy to find out his name. This I did and, although I didn't know why, I felt a moment of disquiet.

In the restaurant I felt his undoubting belief in what he was doing, but a thousand fold in person. But his eyes…

His eyes would seem empty, and then that feeling surged and then they would blaze with a ferocity I couldn't understand. It wasn't hate, love or jealousy. More than anything it was a look of power, of superiority, not in a pompous way, but as if he really did hold the world in his hand. And a feeling that the waiting was almost over.

Although he shone out with nothing but blessing for Haunting Voice, something about that look of withheld power made me shiver.

I berated myself for not listening to my moments of unease before and set out to find out what I could about the Cigar Man.

I found that he was, and always had been, a PR man in several recording companies. He had some ownership rights on certain record labels and odd tracks. Nothing seemed very worrying, just the usual type of man who wants to protect the few interest he has. I found he actively promoted the stuff he owned on a regular basis. He had been growing his portfolio for a good many years.

That's when I turned my attention to the gossips. Half of its wrong, but most cases can be confirmed or denied. Although you don't encourage those you befriend to confide drunkenly to you, there's nothing wrong with priming the local gossips or sour grapes. Like I said, you never pass it around so, when drunk, the gossips trust you, when sober they refuse to gossip because you don't give them any ammo to use against anyone. Somebody with a rightful grudge, no matter how small, can also spill the beans, but usually to back up their own grievance.

I heard a lot of different, possibly conflicting stories, good and bad. But the most intriguing one was from a sound engineer of a recoding studio, talking to a stranger sitting two seats away in his local pub. He nodded in the Cigar Mans direction. There was not only loathing but also a kind of un-admitted fear.

"makesa dead famous and the famous dead," he slurred. "Mada fortune. S'a goal, s'what he is. Not that we see it. Only do all the bloody work."

Having mumbled and slurred his speech, he slid of the stool and headed out the door.

I pondered his words as I made my own way home, but I think, deep down, I had a glimmer of the truth. Or rather, part of it. No way could I have foreseen all of it. I went back to my studies of the public life of the Cigar Man. Looking more closely I realised that a vast majority of his ownership was with deceased artists. Not all, by any means, but enough.

Then I found his name among board members or trustees of some very famous, now demised, stars. Some singers, some writers, one or two actors, a poet, a modern artist. Some had been dead for over sixty years. Some had been barely famous, even obscure, till the Cigar Man took over their rights or PR.

The engineer was right; he did make dead people famous. But he had shares in other acts, still living and breathing. What would happen to haunted voice once true fame was achieved? Was the sound man right? Did the Cigar Man make the famous dead?

Somehow I knew it wasn't as simple as that. In the last two and a half years, HV had released three albums; all considered flops in the big scheme of things. Yet still the Cigar Man had that knowing belief.

Something inside me said I had to be ready to fight this man.

I had never done it before. I had always obeyed my instructions, but I felt that HV was in danger, and that I was adding to it somehow. I must work against my instructions and stop HV achieving fame. I should be a real friend and not a paid one because this was wrong. My job was to solve problems before they arose, this time the employer was the problem. I had only one weapon in this war, myself. The talent I had been employed to use.

I had to turn it full on to the Cigar Man to find out everything. Only then could I know if Hv was in real danger and if so, how to stop it.

HV's next album wasn't being released for another six months, and I knew the Cigar Man felt this to be a very important album in the scheme of things. Though to me it just seemed another collection of slightly sad songs. But it meant HV would be safe for the next six months.

Or so I thought.

That night I called round to HV. The ambulance was already outside. A tragic accident or suicide, no one could say. But I knew.

And I knew what I had to do next.

The Cigar Man *was* a ghoul. He had to be stopped. How I hated myself for not knowing, for not acting sooner. I was just as guilty. I went to him and told him what I knew, that the police would never believe me, so I must solve the problem myself.

The whole time I could feel this happiness and contentment, this relief, almost a glee.

For a moment I doubted his belief that I could be a danger to him. But it wasn't that, he knew he was dead, it was only a matter of time, but he didn't care.

"It doesn't matter. I did it. And there's so much stuff. Session work, unfinished songs, demos, another six albums."

"Ok, but what good will that do you now. You won't be here to promote it. They may get played a few times."

"You think so? Go home and listen again. It's different now. You'll see. I did it."

"Did what?"

"Created the perfect killing machine. They wanted people to die inside hearing those songs, and now they will. Death changes everything. Remember that. It gives birth to the siren."

I must admit, at that point, I just thought he was a rambling lunatic. I put him out of his misery for his own sake, as much as for the safety of others. I cleaned up and went home.

I knew from that moment on I was out of the friend making business. I didn't realise it would be the complete end of *me* as well.

You see, the T.V. and the radio started playing the tracks on HV's new album, and the old stuff. And now it is different. Because now you hear the words knowing the person is dead and realise they are not said, they are prophetic, a knowledge of an unfinished life. The pain of life and death.

It makes me go cold listening to it. It makes me realise how painful life is for everyone and how simple it would be to sleep forever. Because love, future, purity, all will be denied, unknown. So why suffer the pain of living an unfulfilled life.

It penetrates into the soul of those who hear them. It calls with an aching pain, to be played again and again. Around me, in houses, restaurants, trains, TV shops, clothes stores, the people with their headphones and bipods, shed dry silent tears, for the sorrow is so deep, the future so bleak, they all think, why bother? Why not sleep the pain away or let it intensify till the heart bursts and never feels pain again.

And I'm an empath.

I've trained to enhance my senses.

Most of you will be dead in six months.

I won't get through the night.

The Book of Bodies

1
Maneaters

'Gosh, Isn't it wonderful!'
'Yes, it is, now. Of course, all the damage that was done, turned all this area into a dust bowl. Worse. The soil was ninety per cent salt. Anyone caught out here without water was just a few hours from death.'
'Really?'
'Really. If it wasn't for the project, the whole land would have died eventually.'
'It looks like a paradise.'
'That's because it is, of sorts.'
'My husband spoke a lot about the project, but not what it really was. Just 'The Project' and how well it was going.'
'It's simple really. We had three major problems; pollution, water and decimated land. The project managed to solve all three using the same source.'
'Oh yes?'
'Yes. You see there are billions of people on the planet. A couple of million die every week. Cremation and burial were no longer a solution. In towns and cities there was no more room for cemeteries and the crematoriums where constantly belching out swathes of thick black smoke.'
'Gosh, that sounds terrible.'

'It was. The smoke polluted the clouds. Turned them acidic, as well as not allowing the sun to get through, or get through too much, scorching the land.'

'Ah, lack of water.'

'Exactly, but then nature being nature, it tries to compensate and melts the polar caps, causing flooding else where.'

'I didn't know that's what caused it.'

'Oh yeah. The planet is a living thing in it's own right. But most people don't think of it like that.'

'No, I must say, I never have. Strange really. It's a place *of* life, I know, but…'

'It has a heartbeat, veins, I'd say even a mind.'

'My, ha ha.'

'Then, places like this, deforested, water resources elsewhere, was the death of it. No plants, no insects, no wildlife. The land dies.'

'Yes, I can understand that.'

'So we thought, well, all these bodies, full of nutrients and water, all of this land dying because of a lack of both. All that smoke from the crematoriums. It might be mostly invisible, but you are still breathing it in.'

'My, how horrible.'

'Seemed an obvious solution. Plus there's the bonus of re-homing the maneaters.'

'Maneaters?'

'Yeah, well you see in some continents, Africa, Asia, you get the odd Komodo dragon, bear, lion, alligator, that turns to humans. Usually through old age or a wound. Used to just shoot them, but now we repatriate them here. Can't cause any harm but do the world of good in recycling the dead. Not only them, of course. We've got Vultures, buzzards, couple of Dingoes, wild hogs, flesh eating ants and any number of insects and plants that thrive on it. Now this place is so much happier.'

'Yes, er…it certainly looks it.'

'Never seem a place bounce back so well. And the skies around here, and around the cities too. Fair makes you proud it does. Knowing you helped stop such waste.'

'Waste?'

'Of resources. Of course, this isn't the only reclamation park now, but it was the first. We made the world see how it could be.'

'Yes, you certainly did. And I'm sure my husband would be very proud.'

'He was indeed. Loved it he did. Loved the planet and every creature on it. Including you.'

'Yes, he did. I'm a very lucky woman.'

'Yes, you are. You see, we know what you did.'

'I beg your pardon?'

'The old will, the new will. Your husband often talked about what would happen to the park, in the event, like.'

'I don't see…'

'He said you always said you didn't care about the money. Not really. And that you had enough diamonds and furs from your first two husbands, enough to keep you going. (He hated those so much. Dead animals and dead miners, he called them.) But he loved you. He said a little put by would keep you going. The rest for the park, to keep the gates open. Metaphorically of course.'

'Look, my husband may have said those things, but…'

'Not only said them, showed us the paperwork. But you, your diamonds and furs where not enough, were they?'

'I demand that you turn this helicopter around now.'

'no, you wanted it all. You think you can sell off the park, make a fortune. You don't even care who you sell it too, or what they want the land for.'

'I'm serious, you take me back now or…'

'You don't care that all these creatures here, all the trees and plants will be destroyed again. Not you, draped in dead animals and dead miners.'

'That's it, I'll have your job, you're finished.'

'No missus, you are. See, we're about to have a little accident. It's happened before. We'll be ok, but you, you unfortunately suffered a severe injury. You died. In accordance with your last wishes, we left you here. It's well known how enthusiastic you were about your husband's work.'

'You wouldn't dare.'

'Wouldn't we? Funny that. I think we would. I think we'd also dare bringing out the true will. We've got copies. You may have bought off one lawyer. We've bought off three. Take her down Jeff.'

'No, look, stop. Ok, there's been a misunderstanding. I'll split the money with you.'

'Money? MONEY? You think this is about money?'

'Ok, look, you've done a fantastic job. I can see that, anyone can see that. But the trees here are worth their weight in gold. Plus, once the land is cleared, it can be used again. You can start over. If we just sell the logging rights…'

'Is that what they told you? No loggers would come here, they wouldn't last two minutes.'

'Then I don't understand.'

'No. You wouldn't. See, the dead here, they go back to the planet.'

'So you said.'

'Free range, biodegradable, that's us. But those other companies, they might have a little park on top,

something to show how green they are, but underneath they are factories. Factories for making electric, for supplying power. Which they charge for. They're running out of bodies. Why? Cos they charge. They charge to take away, they charge for everything they can. We do it for free. People donate their bodies to us. We collect them, we bring them here end of transaction. They charge to remove, to process the remains, they charge again for the electric, the water, the fats that they're left with. But if every body comes here, they've got nothing.'
'But…I didn't know…I just…'
'Just signed on the dotted line, so you could buy more dead skins and bits of pretty glass.'
'Please.'
'Don't worry, you won't be alone. Your little lawyer friend is down there too. If he made it through the night.'
'You can't do this. It's inhuman.'
'No love, it's very human. Oh, word of advice, it probably won't make much of a difference, but running around down there in a fur coat, not sure I would.'
'Nnnoooooooo…'
'Alright Jeff, take her back up.'

2
Selling Point

'If you'd like to come through here, I can show you the aquarium area.'
'Wow, I've never seen anything like it.'
'Yes. As you can see, the raw product…'

'You mean bodies?'

'Hmm. We don't like to use that term here. After all, some people can feel a little squeamish. It's best not to think of them as our recently departed loved ones. Once they have been processed upstairs…'

'You mean stripped and shaved?'

'*Yes*. Well, *anyway*, they are referred to as raw product. Anyway, each is placed into the first tank. Here we have our biggest carrion eaters. As you can see, the tank has slotted sides and bottom. This allows any fragments to fall through into our first three conveyer tanks. Each tank,\there after, has thinner and thinner slots until you reach the sand banks, which in turn rise upwards to meet the outflow pipes which water the gardens above.'

'What about the bones?'

'The calcium is removed from the first tank once cleaned of any residue. They are then baked using a heating system controlled by the flow of the water tanks. Then they are crushed and then fed into the sand tanks.'

'So it's not really sand in there?'

'Some is. But although you may see some minute creatures, what you can't see with the naked eye is that those sand banks are filled with millions of creatures that feed on the crushed calcium. It also seeps backwards into the other tanks, where it fills the silt trays at the bottom. These also have billions of tiny creatures in them. If you would like to look into the tank via the red circles, these are magnifiers…'

'Oh wow, look at that. Amazing. So, like, do you ever get, like, floating eyeballs and stuff?'

'Most of the nutrient meat is stripped from the calcium in the first tank. It is really best not to think of it as it was in a living tissue.'

'No, I get that. I just thought it must be a bit freaky, you know, looking in the tank and seeing something looking back.'

'*Anyway*, this is the aquarium section. It can process fifty bodies a day per area. This means that four hundred pints of water a day are returned to the planet, just from this area. And we have ten areas, which means a total of four *thousand* pints of water. Plus the calcium and other minerals and nutrients, which feed the gardens above.'

'Those gardens are pretty great, I must say.'

'Yes. This concludes the aquarium section. Soon we shall break for lunch and then this afternoon we will visit the insect areas, which are a real treat, I can assure you. Any questions?'

'Yes. Will you be processed in this way?'

'No sir. I've chosen to be resourced in the bio-gas area.'

'Bio-gas? Isn't that where they cook you and convert you into energy for electric and stuff?'

'It's more complicated than that. But we will visit that area after the insect area, so if I could hold those questions until then.'

'Ok. But why not here, or the insects?'

'Personally believe that it's my responsibility to make sure that others benefit from my death as much as possible. I agree that all our processing areas are good for the planets and good for humans as a rule. I like to think that providing energy for others to use in this world of sky rocketing prices is my way of making sure there is plenty to go around. Gardens are very pretty and give bees somewhere to live. And the insects provide a good basis for composts. But I'd like to do a little more than that. Besides it tickles me to think that when an old lady turns on her TV or a hospital has the power to give a life saving operation to a child, it will be because of me.'

'Wow. That does sound great.'

'Yes. Of course, not everyone feels that way. And as I said, bees need to live ha ha.'

'How did it go?'

'The usual. Three for the garden, seven for the insects, twenty five for the power plant.'

'I don't know how you do it.'

'First rule, never seem like a sales man. I'm just a guy doing a job. Second rule, always show the power plant last. It means they've forgotten the first two.'

'But it's only a show room. That's not what really happens.'

'Don't care. I get a hundred for everyone that signs on that dotted line.'

'And is it really what you would choose?

'No chance. Insect room for me. Consumed in seconds. What about you?'

'Dunno. Either aquarium or insects. I like bees, and gardens. It'd be nice.'

'Yeah, but they don't make anything. They're only there for the green brigade.'

'I guess. But I really don't like the thought of what they do down there.'

'Me neither. Oh well, another day another dollar. See you tomorrow.'

'Yeah. Night mate.'

3
Working Men

'How come no one ever comes down here?'

'Cos no one wants to see it, that's why.'
'Don't see why. I mean we do all the work.'
'Yeah well, it's like restaurants innit.'
'What do you mean?'
'Well, you get dressed up, go out for a steak. You don't want to see how they get the steak do you? I mean, you don't go to the slaughter house. You don't visit the abattoir. No. You just want your steak, cooked, few chips and mushrooms.'
'I s'pose. But still, half their gadgets wouldn't charge if it weren't for us. Couldn't eat in their fancy restaurants if it weren't for us.'
'That ain't the half of it Boyo. They make a bloody fortune form us.'
'How d'you mean?'
'They rake it in, hand over fist. First for disposal costs, then upkeep for the gardens and such. But what those poor blighters don't realise is once they've signed that bit o paper, company can sell the organs an bits that can still be used. Forget how much those needing a donor will pay, the medical research teams will hand over a fortune to those that can insure they get first refusal.'
'Blimey.'
'Yep. Then you got those that want the fat. Let alone the fisheries that want the maggots for fattening up their stocks. It's all back-handers here and hush-hush there.'
'And we do al the work.'
'Yep. Always have. That's how the rich stay rich. Don't want to be down here in the muck and stench. Keep themselves clean. Show a good show and charge every bugger for everything.'
'I heard about this place abroad.'
'You mean the park?'
'Yeah. Just lay the bodies out and animals roaming around eating us. I dunno. Seems weird.'

'What, weirder than skinning, organ removal and hanging up over drip trays, you mean?'

'Yeah, but like at least the heat from it all does something, not just nothing.'

'No Boyo, not nothing. Feeding the land, the planet, not just people's pockets.'

'Yeah, but what if they go mad and escape and start killing everyone?'

'Won't happen. Besides, if it weren't for them, this place would never have started. It all goes round.'

'I guess. So, what about you?'

'What about me?'

'I mean when you, you know, move on?'

'Move on? There's no moving on.'

'I mean like, god and stuff.'

'Listen, if there is a god, you're standing on him right now. What is it they say, God is in everything. Stands to reason then that this planet is god and that's where I'm going.'

'You mean the park? And let all those lions and stuff rip you to shreds?'

'Better a lion than you.'

'Haha. You know I'd do a good job.'

'Yeah, but think on, who's going to do a good job on you?'

'Ah, but by that time they'll have found a cure for everything.'

'Ha ha, yeah, right. Nature finds a way Boyo. Look at the dinosaurs, too many and a bloody great meteor.'

'Yeah, well, that's if I'm still here. Companies talking about starting a processing unit on Mars. There's so many colonists now, they say they want to get their foot in the door, be the first off earth.'

'Where d'you hear that?'

'I've got my ear to the ground, me.'

''Yeah right. Still chatting up that young bit in the canteen?'
'Her name's Heather. And yes, I might. She says she's going places and I've a mind to go with her. People will always need feeding, that's what she says.'
'Yeah, well, she's right. And bodies will always need disposing. So let's get on with it, eh. Unless you're too busy with your space training.'
'I won't need space training, will I. It'll be just like down here with you, but up there.'
'Right. Come on then. Get those frames stripped and those drip trays on seven cleaned. The next batch is due soon.'
'Aye aye captain.'

4
Coming Home

'Charlie Tango Five, coming in to orbit.'
'Roger, Charlie Tango Five. Take it steady. This lot is heading for (****).'
'Isn't that…'
'Yep, where buck house used to be.'
'Weird innit, to think we all came from here? Well, our great grand parents. I remember the pictures of buck house. There was a queen then you know.'
'Yeah, I know.'
'My great grandparents, they worked at the British processing plant that was.'
'Yeah I know, Charlie Tango Five. You tell me every bloody time.'
'Alright, just making conversation. My great Grandad said they had these frames they hung the bodies on after they'd skinned em and removed their organs. He said

the bits would rot off and fall in the drip trays. He said the smell of the maggots that first week killed his nose. Couldn't smell a thing after.'

'Charlie Tango Five, some of us are eating here you knoOw.'

'Sorry. But I mean it's weird innit. To think what they used to do with peoples bodies?'

'Charlie Tango Five, ate you going to make this bloody drop or not?'

'Yeah, 'm just saying. I mean, if they'd carried on with the off world processing, Earth, the planet we came from, would have died. It's nice that it's still here, that we return.'

'Charlie Tango Five, if you don't make that drop, you are going to return a lot quicker than you thought, understood?'

'*Fine*. Charlie Tango Five making drop...Now...Ok?'

'About bloody time. Ok. Charlie Tango Five, you are clear to head back.'

'Cheers, see you soon.'

'Not too soon I hope. Ok, Foxtrot Alpha Two, are you there?'

'Foxtrot Alpha Two, coming in to orbit.'

'Roger Foxtrot Alpha Two. You are heading for (****).

'Hey, isn't that the old Eiffel Tower?'

'Oh for goodness sake.'

5
Old Bodies

'Sigmund, is it true?'
'About Sol's system? I'm afraid so.'
'But...It's where humans began.'

'There's no point in being sentimental, Nadia.'

'But Sigmund…'

'No buts, Nadia. It's prime for mining. We can strip what we need, what can be used elsewhere. Sol is obsolete, has been for a long time. It's only the die hard fanatics that want to give it protected status.'

'But *Sol*. I remember my grandparents talking of Mars and Earth.'

'They are just bodies, Nadia. Dead bodies, no use. But they can help other systems live on.'

'But it happens everywhere. Can't there be just one place that's left untouched?'

'For what purpose? Its too far for people to visit. It doesn't even have modern astro ports. People don't even go there on the way to somewhere else. It's just a group of spinning balls of nutrients, water and minerals. Those things are better off somewhere else, somewhere useful.'

'Oh, Sigmund.'

'Nadia, be sensible. When was the last time you even thought about Sol? No one does, apart from your grandparents. And even they didn't land on any of the planets, just took loads of pictures to bore people with.'

'But what will we tell our grandchildren, what will they tell their grandchildren, about where we came from?'

''We came from Setnos 5, same as our parents did.'

'You have no sense of history.'

'Oh yes I do. Mining is a proud human heritage. It's what we do. We take an old body, reclaim what we can and make our world a better place.'

'I just think there should be some places left, as nature intended.'

'As nature intended? Sol will one day blow up or blow out. Let's get in there before all the useful stuff goes with it.'

'Sigmund…'
'Nadia, People die, planets dies, systems die. It's a fact of life. But humans, as a race, go on. It's our purpose.'
'I suppose, but I still think it's sad.'
'Will you think it's sad when your grandchildren have enough water to buy their own planet? Just as we did?'
'I suppose not.'
'And it takes a lot more than just water these days, Nadia. A lot more.'
'Yes, Sigmund. I know.'
'So, no more about some old dead bodies that are no use to anyone. Ok?'
'Ok, Sigmund.'

Milton Keynes UK
Ingram Content Group UK Ltd.
UKHW040950140324
439439UK00001B/51